# The Great Central Fair:
# A Saint Maggie Story

# The Great Central Fair:
# A Saint Maggie Story

## Janet R. Stafford

Squeaking Pips Press, Inc.
2018

First Printing: 2018

ISBN: 978-0-9992285-6-2

Cover Image from Library of Congress
No known restrictions on publication
See the "Notes & References" section of this book for more information


Squeaking Pips Press, Inc.
Hillsborough, NJ 08844
www.squeakingpips.com

All scripture quotations are from the King James Bible, unless otherwise indicated.

# Dedication

To all who donate their time, their money, and their talents to make this world a better place.

# Contents

# Acknowledgements

I have a wonderful group of beta-readers, who serve as my editing team. They are:

Dan Bush
Laura Wimbrow
Carol Brosen Drews
Carl Suk
Laurie Doscher

You are so important to me and to the books. Many thanks for your willingness to read and comment. I am grateful for your honesty!

# Preface

Maggie's daughters by John Blaine are becoming women, and like any parent, Maggie is hit by the power and inevitability of the passage of time.

For her daughters, Lydia (Liddy) and Frances (Frankie), growing up brings decisions about the direction their lives will take. In the Saint Maggie Series, the girls have wrestled with occupations that are just starting to creak open and admit women: ministry and medicine.

This story, though, focuses on their personal choices regarding the men in their lives. A visit to the Philadelphia Sanitary Fair of 1864 prompts decisions for both Frankie and Lydia. To a lesser degree, Chester Carson, acting as their chaperone, makes a few decisions of his own.

The Great Central Fair is another name for the Philadelphia Sanitary Fair of 1864. When I first encountered the term "sanitary fair," I had no idea what it was. After doing some preliminary research, I learned that such fairs were fund-raisers held across the Union to benefit the United States Sanitary Commission.

According to the New York Public Library's "Guide to the United States Sanitary Commission," the Commission was civilian-run but "authorized by the United States government to provide medical and sanitary assistance to the Union volunteer forces during the United States Civil War (1861-1865)." Eventually the Commission's work was expanded to regular soldiers, sailors, and civilians.

The Sanitary Commission set about doing its work in June of 1861. It was supposed to inspect recruits, "the health and sanitary condition of the volunteer forces, their general comfort and efficiency, the provision of cooks, nurses and hospitals," and related subjects. It also carried out hospital and camp inspections regarding sanitary conditions and food preparation and quality, kept statistics, and issued reports on the same. ("Guide," ii.)

As the war continued, emergency relief in the way of food and nursing help was added to its mission.

Because the U.S. Sanitary Commission was not supported by government funds, raising money for its work was crucial, and that's where the Sanitary Fairs come in. According to the *Philadelphia Sanitary Fair Catalogue & Guide*, the first fair originated in Chicago late in 1863 and raised $80,000. It was followed by fairs in Boston, Cincinnati, Albany, Brooklyn, Buffalo, Cleveland, Metropolitan New York, Baltimore, Saint Louis, Washington (D.C.), and Pittsburgh. (More were scheduled to open after the Philadelphia fair.)

I added the amount of money raised by the fairs mentioned in the *Catalogue & Guide*, and it came to $2,829,661. Think about it. That money came from donations, from average people in the Union during 1863-64. That was a great deal of cash for that era and illustrates how strongly people believed in the United States Sanitary Commission's work with their troops and the nation itself.

Sources
"Guide to the United States Sanitary Commission (1861-1879)." The New York Public Library Manuscripts and Archives Division.
http://archives.nypl.org/mss/3101

*Philadelphia Sanitary Fair Guide and Catalogue.* Thomas Izod, editor. Philadelphia: Magee, Stationer, June 1864.

# Introduction

This novella is part of "the Saint Maggie universe," a family saga set mostly in New Jersey during the mid-1800s.

I never intended to write a historical fiction series. But while I was working on my Ph.D. in North American Religion and Culture, I took a tutorial that dealt with scandals in Methodist ministry. For the required research paper, I found a sad, tragic story about a talented, charismatic young minister named Jacob Harden who lived in Warren County, NJ during the 1850s. Harden ended up in a shotgun marriage, a result of his own charisma and plotting on the part of his future mother-in-law. Predictably, his marriage was not a happy one. And his response was... well, shall we say it did not live up to the expectations one might have of a clergyman?

The story stuck with me long after the paper had been turned in and graded. I often would wonder how it could be fictionalized into a novel. So, a few years after my Ph.D. was granted, I decided to try my hand at telling the story as fiction.

The result was a character-driven tale set in 1860-61 called *Saint Maggie.* The story revolves around a good-hearted, Methodist widow named Maggie who runs a boarding house and receives the new minister, Jeremiah Madison, as her new boarder. The cast of characters in Maggie's house is eclectic: a failed aging writer named Chester Carson; Jim "Grandpa" O'Reilly, an old indigent Irishman; a struggling young lawyer by the name of Edgar Lape; and the undertaker's apprentice, Patrick McCoy. I gave Maggie two teenage daughters: Lydia, the sensible one who has a knack for nursing, and her younger sister Frances (Frankie), the outspoken, opinionated one. Completing the cast are Emily and Nate Johnson. Emily is Maggie's closest friend and the boarding house cook. Nate is a carpenter. The Johnsons are black, which does not sit well with the town folk because they live in Maggie's house, which is right on the town square and it is clear they are friends more than employees. Finally, we have Elijah Smith, who at the time was the editor of a penny weekly called the *Gazette*. A former Quaker and self-proclaimed free-thinker, Eli is sweet on Maggie. We are introduced to their romance and eventual marriage in the first few chapters of the novel.

I became a self-published author in 2011 and released *Saint Maggie* through my micro-publishing company, Squeaking Pips Press, Inc.

I thought *Saint Maggie* would be a single novel and that I would move on to other stories, but one little question changed that. While speaking about my book to book clubs and other groups, people repeatedly asked: "What happens next?" I realized that readers loved the characters and wanted more stories about them.

And that's how I ended up writing a series comprised of novels, short stories, and now a novella about Maggie, her family, and friends, and the issues of and life in 1860s America.

The series is getting quite large, and so is the cast of characters within it. Some come and go for one book, while others are recurring. Early on, I learned to include a cast of characters list in my novels and short stories. That also is the case with this novella. That section follows this one.

I have included a list that shows *The Great Central Fair's* chronological place in the other Saint Maggie stories and novels.

| | |
|---|---|
| "The Dundee Cake" (short story) | 1852 |
| *Saint Maggie* (novel) | 1860-61 |
| *The Enlistment* (novella) | 1862 |
| *Walk by Faith* (novel) | 1863 |
| "The Christmas Eve Visitor" (short story) | 1863 |
| *A Time to Heal* (novel) | 1863 |
| *Seeing the Elephant* (novel) | 1864 |
| *The Great Central Fair* (novella) | 1864 |

# Cast of Characters

| | |
|---|---|
| Maggie Beatty Blaine Smith | Editor, homemaker |
| Lydia Blaine Lape | Maggie's daughter, doctor |
| Frankie Blaine | Maggie's daughter |
| Elijah Smith | Maggie's husband, Editor-in-Chief of the *Register* |
| Bob Smith | the Smiths' son |
| Faith Smith | the Smiths' infant daughter |
| Chester Carson | *Register* reporter, friend, former lodger |
| Birgit Brennan | maid & governess |
| Moira Brennan | maid & cook |
| Nate Johnson | carpenter, friend |
| Emily Johnson | baker, homemaker, friend |
| Natey Johnson | the Johnsons' son |
| Sgt. Patrick McCoy | Frankie's beau |
| Capt. Philip Frost | Lydia's beau |
| Alfred Benning | Owner of the Philadelphia Gallery of Photographic Art |

# Chapter 1: Good News

**1 June 1864**

The door to the *Blaineton Register* flew open; newsboy and general helper Daniel Coopernall stomped into the reception area shouting, "Mail!"

Frowning, Editor-in-Chief Elijah Smith stopped his conversation mid-word with receptionist Andy Randall. He had taken both Danny and Andy off the streets, where they once had a promising career in petty theft and a possible future behind bars. Now they festooned his newspaper office with adolescent shenanigans and high spirits, which he found both amusing and annoying. On this day, Danny's behavior was firmly in the "annoying" category.

"How many times do I have to tell you not to shout in the office?" Eli groused.

"Sorry." But the thirteen-year-old was not the least bit sorry. He grinned, passed the batch of mail to the portly middle-aged man, and clomped off to attend to his second job, helping Mr. Larsen with the rotary press.

Andy laughed. "I don't think he'll ever change, Mr. Smith."

Eli grunted. "Suppose not." His leg was killing him. He leaned against the wall behind the reception desk for extra support. Ever since he had suffered a bullet wound during an incident in 1861, he had been forced to use a walking stick to get around. Somedays he was pain-free. Others, like this one, were uncomfortable. If only he hadn't tried to talk that crazy girl with a gun from firing upon him and his wife. If perhaps he had tried to overpower her instead...

Eli briefly rued the non-violent values instilled in him by his Quaker mother. It was the desire for peace and non-violence that also had caused him to leap between two men in a foolish attempt to stop one from stabbing the other. Eli had received the knife in his side as a reward. Fortunately, the blade was short and his girth wide. As his stepdaughter, physician Lydia Lape so bluntly put it, his fat had saved his life.

"Never again," he muttered, rubbing his side.

"What, sir?" Andy asked.

"Nothing." With a sigh, he pushed his wire rim spectacles up his nose and began sorting through the mail: a thick pile of varied correspondence comprised of newspapers, letters to the editor, bills, and personal mail for himself and his family. As he shuffled through, Eli frowned and lifted one of the pieces.

Andy noticed. "Something wrong?"

"Another letter from Captain Philip Frost. For Lydia."

Eli's oldest stepdaughter, who would turn 22 years in another month, had developed an on-going friendship with Frost and Eli wasn't sure he liked it.

Theoretically, he could understand the relationship. The two had medicine in common. Frost, a doctor in the military, served at Harewood General Hospital in Washington, D.C., while Lydia worked at the new hospital just outside Blaineton with the town's doctor, Frederick Lightner, who was her supervisor and advisor.

Lydia and Frost had had met during the Smith family's sojourn in Gettysburg. As if being chased out of Blaineton by a group of Copperhead* ruffians in 1863 had not been enough, Eli's wife, family, and friends were present in Gettysburg during the battle of July 1-3 and its heart-wrenching aftermath. After the battle, Capt. Frost paid the Smith House a visit. He was charged with

---

* See NOTES & REFERENCES section

moving soldiers from numerous impromptu hospitals – schools, churches, and private homes – to Camp Letterman General Hospital, a new, temporary facility built just outside the town. Frost made friends with Lydia, who had been taking care of the wounded lodged in the Smith house.

Despite the many things the two young people had in common, Eli found the relationship between Lydia and the Captain to be a head-scratcher. After all, Lydia's husband Edgar had been killed only a year ago at Chancellorsville. From all indications, she still was in mourning. Furthermore, she and Frost had fought like cats and dogs while in Gettysburg once the Captain suspected that a Confederate soldier, who had been in Lydia's care, was missing.

The resulting bruhaha was one Eli wished he could forget, mainly because the controversy and confusion had resulted in him being thrown in jail and hauled up before the District Provost Marshal.

Fortunately, imprisonment and/or hanging were the bullets Eli had managed to dodge when the case was dismissed.

After the dust had settled, Lydia and Philip were able to mend their disagreements. Now Frost seemed to be pursuing her romantically.

Eli could understand that, too. His stepdaughter was an intelligent young woman and a gifted physician. It also didn't hurt that she had shiny coffee-colored hair, deep brown eyes, a fetching smile, and a curvy figure.

Yes. Frost's attraction to Lydia was clear. It was Lydia's response that baffled Eli. She appeared to be holding the Captain off with one hand and beckoning him with the other.

Eli took his position as a stepfather seriously – sometimes too seriously according to his wife Maggie.

7

She claimed that he didn't know when to intervene and when to step back.

However, Lydia was legally an adult, so Eli generally followed a "her business is her business" policy.

With a resigned sigh, he placed the letter on top of mail from his sister Becky and a packet for the family from friend Matilda Strong, a woman who had lived with them after freeing herself and her daughter Chloe from slavery in Virginia. Matilda had been reunited with her husband and sons, and now she and Chloe lived with them in Canada.

"Well," Eli mumbled to no one in particular, "I don't know. Two letters from Frost in two weeks. Who knows what that means?" He pushed his wire-rim glasses back up on his nose.

He lifted the final letter. But when he read the address, he exploded. "Oh, Egad!" And he angrily slapped it on top of the pile.

"Ah," Andy observed, "is that from Patrick McCoy?"

"It is," Eli said between clenched teeth. "And it's for Frankie."

Frankie, whose given name was Frances, was Maggie's youngest daughter from her marriage to the late John Blaine. Headstrong, outspoken, redheaded, and impulsive, the young woman would turn eighteen in a few days. She was the one Eli worried most about.

In 1862, Frankie had cut off her hair, donned men's clothing, traveled to Camp Fair Oaks in Flemington, and attempted to pass as a boy, join the army, and fight at new-recruit Patrick's side.

Fortunately, Patrick had managed to talk some sense into her, and when Eli and Maggie finally arrived in Flemington, they did not have to do any convincing. Their errant daughter was already wanting to go home.

Even though that escapade had proved to Eli that Patrick possessed a bit of common sense, he kept an eye on the young man, just to be safe.

"Well," Eli allowed, "I shouldn't complain. He's been promoted to Sergeant. The fella's got some sense and talent. But, does he need to write Frankie a letter every day? That's madness! When I was a war correspondent, I didn't write to *Mrs. Smith* that often!"

His own words immediately called up the tension that had plagued his marriage in 1863, and he felt a pang of regret. "Maybe I *should* have written to her more." Then he added, bitterly, "Or maybe I should have just stayed home."

"Mr. Carson says that's water under the bridge and you should let it go, Mr. Smith."

Eli's dark eyebrows knit in a frown over his brown eyes. "Really? And how is it Mr. Carson feels free to discuss my life with you?"

Andy shrugged. "I dunno."

"No, you wouldn't, would you?" The truth was Dr. Stanley at the hospital had given Eli the same counsel. He realized that Carson, who was like a brother to him, was probably right. It was flattering that his friend was concerned, but to talk it over with a pup of a boy? What was wrong with that man?

Eli grunted to himself. He'd just have to take that up with Carson. Of course, Carson would only give him a withering look, so what was the use? Why waste the time and the energy?

"Why're you so upset with Patrick, anyhow?" Andy persisted. "He and Frankie are in love. Have been for a long time."

Telegrapher and reporter, Edward Caldwell – a bespectacled young black man – suddenly poked his head through the window that connected his office with

9

the reception room. "I agree, Mr. Smith. You can't stop *that* romance. It's a runaway train."

"Who asked you?" Eli grunted.

"Sorry, sir, but your conversation carried into my office."

Eli sniffed. "You didn't have to listen to it, did you?"

"Some things can't be helped, Mr. Smith."

"Huh. That so? Well while I'm apparently spilling the corn to everyone in this place, let me finish with this: I don't want Frankie running away from home again or doing anything untoward until she and Patrick are legally married."

The two young men guffawed.

"Good luck, Mr. Smith," Andy joked, "You're talking about Frankie."

Edward grinned. "She does have a mind of her own, sir."

"I know. I just hope she doesn't break her mother's heart, that's all. Conversation over." Eli tucked the letters in his jacket pocket. "Andy, go get the others, it's time for dinner."

#

Greybeal House, located just outside of Blaineton, New Jersey, had been home to the Greybeal family since the 1700's and had grown with the family's size and prosperity, until it was comprised of the original wing (built of local stone in 1732), and two wooden additions, built in 1816 and 1840.

Recently, the Greybeal family had moved to other locales, leaving only old Mrs. Greybeal in the cavernous building. When her son insisted that she come to Trenton to live with him and his family, the old mansion went up for sale.

Seeing her chance, Tryphena Moore, owner of the *Blaineton Register* and ally of Eli and Maggie, purchased the home with money from the sale of the lot on which Maggie's boarding house had once stood.

Now the old place once again was filled with life. Not only did Eli, Maggie, Lydia, and Frankie live there, but so did Eli and Maggie's son Bob and baby daughter Faith. Maggie's good friends and co-workers from her boarding house days, Nate and Emily Johnson, and their son Natey also resided in the house. Many of the town folks were bothered by the Johnsons' color (they were black) and by the fact that they had always been considered family to Maggie. A minority of the white people in town regarded Maggie as "eccentric" in her affection toward her dark-skinned friends but let sleeping dogs lie, especially once Nate re-started his carpentry and wheelwright business. The truth was everyone in town knew he was best in the county and were only too happy to go to him for their cabinets, tables, wheels, and such.

But the eccentric world of Greybeal House also was home to James "Grandpa" O'Reilly, an old man of no fixed job, and Chester Carson, a failed writer of fiction who had found new life as Eli's assistant editor and chief reporter. Added to the mix was boarder and reporter Edward Caldwell, as well as two maids: Moira Brennan, who also assisted Emily and Maggie with the cooking, and Birgit Brennan, who served double duty as the younger children's governess. True to form, Maggie treated all her boarders and employees as family.

Despite the controversy and the whispers on the outside, life inside Greybeal House was congenial.

It was so much so that Eli had completely forgotten he had his family's mail stuffed in the pocket of his jacket until noonday dinner was over and he was about to go out the door.

11

"Oh!" He pulled the packets out. Like Eli, they now were somewhat rumpled. "Say, Maggie! Got some letters. One's for Frankie, one's for Liddy, and one is for my lovely wife and her dear friend Emily."

Maggie received her mail and read the return address. "Why, it's from Matilda Strong! I haven't heard from her in months. I'll take it upstairs and read it to Emily after we're done cleaning up."

"How's the lying-in coming along?" Eli asked.

Maggie affectionately rolled her eyes. "It's hardly a lying-in. Emily keeps getting up and insisting on working."

Eli grinned. "Well, if she's doing that, then I imagine Nate and Emily's next baby will be here soon."

"Not quite. It's just neither of us quite know how to lie-in properly. Lounging about in bed all day seems a waste of time, something we never could afford until this year."

Eli picked up Patrick's letter and, with a resigned clearing of his throat, said, "Here's the one for you, Frankie."

She immediately was at his side and plucking the packet out of his hand. "Oh, goody," she chirped. "It's from Patrick!" She eagerly scampered to the sitting area to read the missive in private.

Maggie's oldest daughter Lydia was striding toward the kitchen's door when Eli called, "Got a letter for you, too, Liddy."

Lydia turned. "For me?" She took it from her stepfather and glanced at the name on the return address. "Captain Frost? He never writes more than once a week. I wonder what's going on?" But she tucked it into her black medical bag. "I'll just have to read it later. I need to check in at the hospital." She gave her mother a kiss on the cheek. "Goodbye, Mama." Turning to Eli, she said, "May I ride along in the wagon?"

12

"Of course."

"Thank you. I would like to take it to the hospital if you don't mind. I promise I'll bring it back to the *Register* no later than six o'clock. I'm not on call tonight."

"Thank goodness for that," Eli teased. "We don't see you enough these days."

Chester Carson smiled warmly at Lydia. "Nor do we want you wearing yourself out. You must take good care of yourself for the sake of your patients."

"Don't worry about me, Mr. Carson," was her brisk reply.

"I suppose not." Carson laid a hand on her arm. "There's no need to return the wagon, my dear. We'll walk back to Greybeal House. It's a beautiful day and it promises to continue into the evening."

Eli's sigh caught Carson's notice. He glanced curiously at his friend.

"It's just..." Eli began. "Well... my leg..."

Nate spoke up. "I'll come and get you, Eli."

"But you'd have to hitch up the buggy."

The tall, dark skinned man smiled. "That's no trouble. I'll be looking for a little air by then, anyway. I'm finishing an order of wheels for the carriage manufactory."

"Thank you, friend."

"My pleasure."

Eli gave Maggie a peck on the lips. "See you this evening, sweetheart."

No sooner had the *Register* staff and Lydia gone out the door than Frankie shrieked. "Mama!!"

Alarmed, Maggie nearly tripped over her skirts rushing to her daughter's side. "Good heavens! What is it?"

"He's coming here! He's coming *home*!"

"Who's coming home? Patrick?"

13

"Yes! Patrick!" Frankie now was hopping up and down like an excited puppy.

Maggie heaved a relieved sigh. "Then Patrick hasn't been injured..."

"No, not in the least! He's perfectly healthy." Frankie finally brought her excitement under control. "But he *has* been promoted to sergeant! And, Mama, here's the best news: his surgeon recommended him for an opening at Mower U.S. General Hospital. He's coming to Philadelphia. He's going to be a steward!"

"What's a steward?"

"Well... it's a... a..." Frankie frowned. "I don't know."

Maggie put a hand on her daughter's arm. "Don't worry. I'm sure we'll find out as soon as Patrick gets here."

"He says he's coming for a visit on Monday and he'll have a week's leave before he reports for duty." Frankie's eyes abruptly filled with tears. "Oh, Mama! He'll finally be away from the fighting!" She pulled a handkerchief from the sleeve of her dress and scrubbed her eyes. "Oh, I'm so happy! I've been terribly afraid this whole while..." And she burst into sobs.

Maggie put her arms around her daughter and pulled her close. "I know, my dear. This is welcome and wonderful news, and such a relief. Cry all you want."

#

That evening, everyone had finished supper and was sitting on the porch when the family's carriage came up the drive with Lydia at the reins.

Nate and Carson stood up and stepped off the veranda to meet her and take care of the horse.

Smiling, Lydia thanked them and, black physician's bag in hand, strode smiling across the drive. Her mother met her part way and gave her a hug and kiss.

14

"How was the hospital?" Maggie asked as they strolled arm in arm to the kitchen.

"A bit tricky. We had an issue with a young boy who presented with appendicitis. Dr. Lightner performed the appendectomy while I assisted. It was a good thing we did it. The appendix was ready to rupture. We got it out in time, though."

"I'm glad to hear it went well," Maggie said. "The boy's family must be relieved." They entered the inviting old kitchen with its white, plastered walls. A black range and walnut cupboards sat at one end, and an enormous fireplace and sitting area at the other, separated by a substantial dining table in the middle.

Maggie said, "We had cold beef hash with bread, fresh asparagus, a cold potato salad, and rice pudding for dinner. Would you like me to fix you a plate?"

"I'm not very hungry. I would like to have some of the hash on a piece of bread, though."

"Of course." Maggie went to the icebox and retrieved the bowl. "Would you care for some of the asparagus, as well?"

"That sounds good." Lydia fetched a plate and silverware from the Dutch cupboard. As she set the utensils on the table, she commented, "I read Captain Frost's letter while I was at the hospital. He says he will be sent to Mower General Hospital."

Maggie nearly dropped the bread board she was holding. "Mower? Is that right?" She brought the board over and set it and a half-loaf of bread on the table. "That's where Patrick is going, too."

"Is he?" Lydia's face lit up. "How wonderful! They'll both be away from the fighting. I can't believe our good fortune."

"Will the Captain be able to stay with us before he reports?"

"Yes. He says he'll be here on the sixth of June."

15

Maggie brought the bowl of hash and a spoon over. "I'm sure you, Frankie, Patrick, and the Captain will have a good visit."

"It should be quite jolly," Lydia agreed. She spread hash over a piece of bread and began to devour it.

"Lydia do sit down, please. It isn't good for the digestion to eat standing up."

With the slightest of sighs, Lydia sank onto a chair.

Maggie followed suit. "Liddy..."

"Mm?" her daughter replied around a mouthful of hash sandwich.

"Do you think Captain Frost is fond of you?"

A pair of wide, brown eyes met Maggie's. "Well, of course. We're friends."

"No. I mean..." Maggie took a breath. "I mean, fond as in interested?"

"Oh, Mama..." Lydia presented her with a composed smile. "This isn't a time to think of that."

"No. I suppose not. I mean, he is still in the army. Do you know when he will be mustered out?"

"No."

"So, you haven't made any plans or had any discussions?"

Lydia chuckled. "Mama! Of course not. We're friends. That's all. Anyway, if we were to make any decisions at all, it would be after the war is over."

"I suppose so," Maggie allowed.

"It is the common-sense thing to do." Lydia flashed a grin at her mother. "For goodness sake, Mama, I'm not Frankie. I don't launch surprises at you every five minutes."

That was true. Lydia was loaded with common-sense. Down-to-earth and logical, she was nothing like her mercurial younger sister.

Maggie smiled at her eldest. "Yes. You've almost always been predictable."

"There. You have nothing to worry about." Lydia tore into the sandwich once again.

# Chapter 2: Patrick

**6 June 1864**

With a pounding heart, Frankie stood on the platform in the late afternoon sun and watched the steam puff closer and closer over the distant trees. In a few minutes, Patrick would be with her again. Her Patrick. The boy she had always loved.

Her body tensed as the black engine emerged from the woods and began its approach to the Blaineton depot. She heard the brakes squeal as it slowed down.

Frankie had worn her best dress for Patrick. It had small, white flowers printed on a green background. He always said he liked the way she looked in green, what with her bright red hair. That hair had been tucked into a neat bun (or as neat as she could get it) and was hidden under an emerald bonnet. However, she knew it was liable to escape any minute and prayed Patrick would get off the train soon.

For appearance's sake, she had donned a corset and several petticoats for the occasion, but she left the crinoline carriage at home. She knew she was going to hug Patrick and couldn't risk having her hoops lift the back of her skirt into the air and give everyone on the platform a view of her drawers.

Frankie's mother and stepfather stood supportively beside her, Maggie was all smiles and Eli preparing himself to be the paternal defender of his stepdaughter's purity.

Maggie's smile, however, hid her mixed feelings. She had known Patrick since he came to town in November of 1857. He was 14 (nearly 15), the undertaker's apprentice, and sleeping in the back of the shop with half-made coffins. Her heart went out to him, since Lydia was only a year older than the boy. Maggie took him in and gave him free room and board until he was able scrape up a few pennies for the rent.

Now that boy, to whom she had been like an aunt, and her youngest daughter appeared headed for the altar.

Faith, supported in a shawl wrapped from Maggie's right shoulder to her left hip, gurgled and stuck a fist in her mouth. Reflexively, Maggie placed a hand on Faith's bonneted little head and gave her a kiss. Would time pass this quickly with the baby? Her heart ached for the years gone by and was afraid to consider the future.

As for Eli, part of him wished the young couple would just get it over with and tie the knot so they could behave as nature dictated and he could relax. But when he glanced at Faith, he wondered if he would have the strength to protect her from the less savory members of the male sex. With any luck, little Fay would be like Lydia.

Eli never had any qualms about his oldest stepdaughter. She had been married, and did it in the usual, proper way. Now she was a widow and that meant she understood the ways of love and sex, and because she also was a doctor, she knew that sex could lead to conception. He was comfortable with her friendship with Capt. Frost. There was nothing to worry about there. Lydia wasn't the problem. Frankie was.

*Impulsive little imp*, he thought and yet couldn't help smiling with deep affection. Frankie drove him mad but could melt his heart with a word. He wondered what kind of an effect Faith would have on him when she reached her teen years. Already he was putty in her chubby little hands. Not a good sign.

Bell clanging and steam hissing, the train eased its way up to the platform and jerked to a halt. Frankie's

19

eyes swept up and down the cars as people alighted and were greeted by family or friends.

Suddenly her expression grew bright. Frankie broke into a run, dodging in and out and around the other people on the platform and ran straight into Patrick's arms.

The tall young man in the blue uniform grabbed his girl up and kissed her full on the lips. Neither he nor Frankie cared what the people around them were thinking. Anyway, ever since the war everyone had grown used to seeing displays of affection in public spaces.

"Oh, Pat," she sighed. "How I've missed you!"

"I've missed you, too, honey. Gosh, it's good to see you."

They hugged for a long moment. When they parted, Frankie grabbed her beau's hand. "Come see Mama and Papa!"

They hurried down the platform to where Maggie and Eli were waiting.

Maggie opened her arms wide as Patrick stepped up to her. As they hugged, she asked, "How was your trip?"

He laughed as he stepped back. "Fine. Didn't hear a single gunshot or cannon." Turning his blue eyes to Frankie's stepfather, he asked, "How're you doing, Eli?"

The two men had spent a great deal of time on the battlefield together – Eli as a correspondent and Patrick as a soldier. The experience had dissolved their formality and they referred to each other by their first names.

Although Eli preferred that people call him by his first name, he did wish Patrick were not quite so free and easy. It was difficult being Frankie's stepfather and having a nearly-equal relationship with the young man.

But he said, "I'm hale and hearty, Patrick."

The two clasped hands, both squeezing hard and ending in a robust shake. Eli tried to impress the younger man with his seniority. Patrick tried for a show of youthful strength. Neither won, and the wrestling match ended.

"So, you're going to be a steward, eh?" Eli.

"Yep. I'll be assisting the doctor as he makes his rounds, giving the patients medicine, and learning as much as I can." He grinned at Frankie. "The surgeon at the field hospital says I have what it takes to be a doctor."

"I knew that all along!" Frankie gazed adoringly at her beau.

"Well, I wouldn't have gotten as far as I have if it were not for Dr. Lightner and the surgeons in the field hospitals."

Eli and Maggie exchanged glances, both of which telegraphed to the other that Patrick was turning into a fine young man with a vocational goal. Maggie's eyes said she was delighted, and Eli's said, "not so fast."

Maggie turned to the young couple. "Shall we go home?"

The younger people nodded and, as they walked away from the train, Patrick asked, "What's Greybeal House like?"

"You'll see," Frankie replied. "And you'll love it just like we do!"

#

Patrick's eyes grew wide the instant he saw the white, weathered but majestic façade of Greybeal House. His eyes took in the two-story Federal-style building with its newer wing to the right and old two-story stone structure to the left.

"Golly! I heard about this place but never walked out here to see it. It's a wonder."

"A slightly creaky wonder, though." Eli clumsily launched himself out of the carriage and using his cane

21

pegged his way to Maggie's side, where he offered a hand to help her down. "But we've repaired the worst of the creakiness. Now the trick is keeping it up."

Maggie said, "Yes. We have hired two young maids to help with the cleaning and cooking."

"One works as our governess, too," Frankie chirped in.

"Governess?" Patrick said and then teased, "We really are coming up in the world!"

He hopped easily out of the carriage and strode over to give Frankie a hand down, even though they both knew she was perfectly capable of doing so herself. It was a polite gesture, like holding the door open, and Patrick relished the opportunity to treat Frankie like a queen. He swept her out of the carriage, turned her around, and set her gently on the ground.

No sooner had he taken his hands from her waist than Natey and Bob barreled down the lane on bare feet and slid to a halt in front of him.

"Hey, Bobby!" Patrick picked the boy up and gave him a hug, despite his being covered in dirt. When he released Bob, he scooped Natey up and hugged him. "It's so good to see you, Natey!"

"What have you two been doing?" Maggie never could figure out how small boys got so thoroughly dirty.

Bob grinned at her. "We're building a fort behind the garden, Mama. We found some old bricks and got a bunch of sticks. Now we can pretend we're fighting the Johnnies."

"Oh, Robert, must you play war?"

"Mama, Natey and me 're *good soldiers!*"

"That's Natey and *I* are good soldiers," Eli corrected. He met his wife's eyes. "Maggie, I think we need to accept that these days boys are going to play war, whether we like it or not."

"Well, I hope they never have to *be* soldiers." Realizing what she had said, Maggie turned to Patrick. "I didn't mean... it's just... I hope you did not take my words the wrong way..."

He smiled. "Not in the least, Mrs. Smith. I understood your meaning." He squatted down on his heels, so he could see the boys' faces. "I hope you fellas never have to be soldiers, either, no matter how exciting it is to play war."

Impressed at Patrick's response, Eli excused himself and took the horse and carriage into the barn. Bob and Natey, meanwhile, dashed back to their fort and Maggie brought the young couple in through the mansion's main entrance.

Patrick gaped at the sweeping stairway and wide, elegant hall.

"That is the library." Maggie indicated a room to their right. "Go through it and you'll find the newest wing, which has a music room on the first floor and four guest rooms above. You shall be staying there."

"Oh, Mrs. Smith..." Patrick sighed. "You mean I'll have privacy? And peace and quiet? I never thought I'd have any of that again!"

As they proceeded down the hall, Frankie pointed out the formal front parlor to their left. Further down was the family's back parlor, and on the right a spacious dining room.

"We were told this was where the Greybeal family held summer and winter balls." Turning, Frankie aimed a pert grin at her beau. "Perhaps this dining room might host a wedding party someday."

"Someday," he replied, grinning back.

Mixed feelings washed over Maggie again. She was happy her daughter and Patrick were speaking of marriage but did not want to consider the notion of Frankie leaving Greybeal House. But she pulled herself together and said, "The bedrooms for the family are above this floor and also above the kitchen."

She led them next through a small hallway. "Through here is our kitchen and sitting area. We use this room much more than we do the formal rooms in the big part of the house."

Patrick took in the kitchen and the cozy sitting area with the immense fireplace. "This looks older than the other parts of the house. It was the first place the Greybeals built, wasn't it?"

"Yes," Maggie replied. "At first, it was only this floor. But when they began to prosper, the family added a second floor to be used as sleeping quarters."

"That's where I sleep," Frankie piped in.

The Brennen sisters, already busily preparing the evening supper, were working a stew of beef and vegetables, as well as biscuits, honey, and cheese. For dessert, they had made berry pies with cream.

They stopped what they were doing and, curious to see Patrick, presented themselves, standing side by side next to the dining table.

"These young ladies are Birgit and Moira Brennan," Maggie explained. "Ladies, may I introduce Sergeant Patrick McCoy."

Both girls curtseyed prettily.

Moira said, "Pleased to meet you, Sergeant."

"Pleased to meet you," he answered. "And call me Patrick, please."

Moira was poised to ask a question but was interrupted by Eli, who burst in the kitchen door. "What's for supper?" He took a deep sniff. "Mm! Beef stew, if I don't miss my guess."

"Yes, Mr. Smith," Birgit replied. "'Tis that. We know it's your favorite and used Mrs. Smith's recipe."

Eli pegged his way over to Patrick. "Why don't I show you to your room, so you can get settled?" He glanced at Maggie. "What room is it, Mrs. Smith?"

"The first room on the right after you climb the stairs from the music room."

Eli motioned for Patrick to follow. The young soldier picked up his haversack and trailed after the middle-aged man.

Frankie frowned as she watched them go. "*I* was going to show Pat his room."

"You know that would not be proper," Maggie clucked. "You're both adults and must maintain a sense of propriety."

"But I know right from wrong."

"I know you do, but it still would not be proper."

As her mother turned to help the Brennen sisters with the meal, Frankie grumbled, "I hate being an adult. It's all about following rules."

#

After supper was over and everything was cleaned up and put away, Frankie wandered outside to the veranda on the front of the house, where she found Patrick sitting alone. She heaved a sigh of relief.

It seemed everyone had wanted to talk to him at supper and she scarcely had been able to say more than a few sentences to him, which was disconcerting and discouraging. Patrick was *her* beau, after all. Why couldn't everyone give them a bit of time together?

Fortunately, for once family and friends appeared to be occupied. Smiling, she strode to where Patrick was seated in a rocking chair. An empty chair was beside him and Frankie plopped down onto it.

"Is it good to be home?" she asked.

"Yes." He smiled warmly at her.

25

She thought he had such beautiful blue eyes. They were deep blue, the way she imagined the sea must look.

"But…"

"But what?" she asked.

"But I miss the old boarding house."

Frankie sighed. "Me, too." A moment of silence passed, then she laid a hand on his arm. "Pat?"

"What?"

"No matter where we live, I'll always love you."

Peepers were calling from a stream while crickets chirped in the dark beyond the porch. It was a familiar and comfortable sound for them both and brought back memories of sitting and talking on the porch at the old boarding house.

Patrick took her hand in his. "I'll always love you, too. No matter where we are."

Frankie relaxed against the back of the rocker. "What should we do next?"

"Next?" He laughed softly. "I go to Mower Hospital, that's what."

"No, I mean…" She took a deep breath and then forged on. "I mean, what should *we* do?"

Patrick let the night sounds speak for a while. Finally, he said, "Frankie, are you talking about marriage?"

"I am."

"Well, I was thinking we could have the wedding once I get mustered out."

She looked so aghast that he had to hold back delighted laughter. He loved, and had missed, her exaggerated responses.

"Pat, that won't be for another year!"

"Aw, honey… It's not forever." He tugged on her arm. "Stand up."

When she did, he patted his lap. "Have a seat."

"Pat!" She was scandalized. "What would Mama say?"

26

"Nothing. Your Mama isn't out here. Neither is Eli."
He chuckled. "If he were, we'd both know it because he'd
be beating me with his cane." He patted his lap again.
"Come on. Sit down. We need to talk."

Pleased, Frankie curled up in his arms.

Patrick kissed the top of her head. "Listen, honey, it
wouldn't be much of a life for you if we got married now.
I'm going to be living and working at Mower. Where
would you stay? In a little room in a Philadelphia
boarding house? With your mother in Blaineton? That
wouldn't be any kind of marriage."

She sighed. "I know. But it's so hard to wait."

They sat for a while, enjoying their time together in
the anonymity of the night.

Suddenly Frankie said, "Pat..."

"What?"

"I think you ought to know something. I just don't
want to be a wife. I want to be a minister."

"You mean a minister in a church?"

She shifted so she could look him in the face. "What
other kind of minister is there?"

Patrick grinned. "Frankie, I swear you're full of
surprises! I didn't even know women *could be* ministers."

"They can't. At least, not yet. But I talked to Papa and
he said..." She was almost afraid to speak it aloud. "He
said I ought to go out west because they need ministers
there and things aren't as... stuffy as they are here."

"That's true." Patrick gave her a kiss and looked
deeply into her green eyes. "You know, they need doctors
out west, too."

"We both could work in a little town out there.
Wouldn't that be fine?"

"It won't be like it is here, though," he said. "Some of
those towns are barely civilized."

"That's why they need us!"

27

Smiling, he gave her another kiss. "I can see that. I'd be their doctor and you would be their minister. One thing's for sure – we'd be the talk of the town, civilized or not!"

Frankie put her head on his shoulder. "I wouldn't care because I'd be with you."

"You need to think long and hard about that. You'd be moving far away from your family. You wouldn't be able to hop on a train and come home whenever you felt like it."

This sobered her. "It's going to be hard and I know I would miss them all terribly."

Patrick tightened his arms around her. "Yeah. Me, too.... But you know what? The good news is we're going make our own family."

She sat up and put a hand to his face. "Oh, Pat, I love you so! Any other man would say I was mad."

"You're not mad. Not in the least. If you say you want to be a minister, then there's a good reason for it."

She leaned against him, resting her head on his shoulder once again. "There *is* a good reason. It's God. I believe God has been calling me for a long time. And it's hard to say no to God."

"It must be. I mean, it's God."

"I guess you're right. We should wait a while before we get married. I need time to adjust to the idea of being without my family. And I'll need to get more experience as a minister, even if no one thinks I should be one. Mr. Lowry wants me to assist him at the hospital. I did it before the trouble started there."

"What trouble?"

"I told you. The riot. They took me as a hostage."

Patrick winced. "How do you get yourself in those situations, Frankie?"

She shrugged. "I don't know. I was trying to get Martha Stroud out of the building and they caught us."

"Well, try not to do that kind of thing so much after we get married and move west."

"I'll try." She grinned. "Hey, Pat..."

"What?"

"Listen to us. We're planning a life together."

He snuggled her. "So, we are."

"Sorry to intrude," an all-too-familiar voice said.

Startled, the young people looked up.

At the sight of her stepfather, Frankie squeaked and leaped to her feet. "Papa! We... uh... we... we were just..."

"I can see what you were 'just'." His eyes rested accusingly on Patrick. "What have you to say for yourself, young man?"

"Nothing. It's all completely innocent."

"Really? Doesn't look that way to me." Eli turned to Frankie. "Go inside, please, Frances. I need to have a word with this fella."

"Papa, please don't –"

"Frances, I asked you to go inside."

Frankie heaved an irritated sigh and, straightening her spine, marched past Eli and into the house.

Once they were alone, Eli pegged his way across the porch and stopped in front of Patrick.

"You don't need to treat her that way, Eli. She's not a child anymore."

"How do you mean, 'not a child anymore'?"

"I mean, she's eighteen years old. She went through the battle at Gettysburg. She served in two field hospitals. She worked in an insane asylum and lived through a riot!"

Eli pursed his lips. "And that's what you mean by 'not a child'?"

"For God's sake, Eli, she only was sitting on my lap!"

"And we both know what *also* is on your lap, don't we?"

Casting his eyes heavenward, Patrick gestured for a little help from a higher authority. Then, with a sigh, he indicated the rocking chair beside his. "Take a seat, Eli."

Eli sank onto the chair, put his cane on the floor, and waited.

Patrick took a big breath. "You need to understand something: I respect Frankie. No, I don't merely respect her, I love her, and I never would do anything to hurt her. Do you remember when I was wounded last year, and she ran away to bring me home from Mower?"

Eli nodded. "Do I? I was mad with worry."

"Well, you would have been even madder if you had known the whole story."

"Oh, yeah? Let's see how mad I get. Tell me."

"Fine. On the way home, the train had stopped in York overnight, so we found an inn. The landlady thought we were married and gave us one room with one bed."

"Why, you miserable little son of a –"

Patrick cut him off. "Nothing happened, Eli!"

The middle-aged man's expression went from anger to confusion. "Nothing? Really?"

"Yes. Nothing. It's not that I wouldn't have liked it, but I know what could have gone wrong. So, we slept in our clothes, side by side. I didn't lay a hand on her. Honest."

"Huh..." That was followed by a long silence. Finally, Eli repentantly said, "Well, young fella, it seems I've misjudged your character."

"I know what's right and wrong, regardless of what you may suspect."

"And I understand the temptations you face." Eli sat back in his chair. "When I was courting Mrs. Smith, we had a moment when... well, let's just say it would have been easy to forget ourselves. I didn't want her feeling guilty or having to explain anything to anyone, so I put a

30

halt to the activity. My meaning is this: I'm glad you exercised restraint because it's easy to get carried away, especially when you've had experience with women."

"Actually, I find it's easier not to get carried away when you haven't had any experience at *all*."

There was dead silence.

"What?" Leaning toward him, Eli whispered, "Are you? I mean, are you saying that...?"

"I am. I'm a virgin. Like Frankie."

Mouth agape, Eli searched for an appropriate response but settled for a chuckle instead. "Damn! And I here I thought –"

"Well, you thought wrong. You even didn't bother to get your facts straight, did you?"

Eli laughed again. "Damn! That's just bell-fired bad journalism on my part, isn't it? Shame on me! Please accept my apology, Patrick." He held his hand out.

Smiling, Patrick shook with him. "Apology accepted, Eli."

"I'll ease up on you from now on. It was nothing personal. I just wanted to make sure Frankie –"

"You love her like a father, don't you?" the young man interrupted.

"Yeah." Eli sat back in his chair. "Yeah, I do."

"Know what I think?"

"What?"

"I think you're not as tough as you act."

"You do, eh? Well, don't let that get around."

"It's our secret."

After another pause, Eli glanced thoughtfully at Patrick. "Say... no one's in the kitchen at this hour."

"So?"

"So, I happen to know where the whiskey bottle is kept." Eli assumed a naughty grin. "Care for a sip or two?"

"Won't Maggie or Emily notice when they go to make a cake or medicine or something?"

"Of course. They always notice. The men sneak sips, the women see the liquor level has gone down, but they never say anything unless they think it's going down too fast." Eli launched himself onto his feet. "Come on, son."

"Son? Say, does that mean...?"

"Hell, no! I don't want to give you a swelled head, do I?"

Laughing, Patrick followed the portly man inside.

# Chapter 3: Philip

**7 June 1864**

Maggie and the Brennan sisters were cleaning up
after breakfast. Everyone had eaten and went about their
business, except Lydia, who was still in bed. Maggie had
chosen not to wake her. Such a busy young woman
needed her sleep. Lydia kept irregular hours and her
work at the hospital was demanding.

The last dish had been dried when Lydia strode into
the kitchen. Maggie couldn't help but notice the frown on
her face. When she asked what was wrong, her daughter
heaved a sigh and sat down. "I've heard nothing from
Captain Frost since his last letter. He said he would be
arriving today."

Moira asked, "Would you care for some tea, Doctor?
My mam always says a good cup of tea can help you sort
anything out."

"I'd love some tea. Thank you."

As Moira went to fetch the pot, Lydia said, "He hasn't
sent a wire. I wonder if perhaps he has changed his
mind."

Maggie placed a hand on her oldest daughter's
shoulder. "I doubt that."

Moira came to the table and poured Lydia a cup,
while Birgit brought the sugar and pitcher of milk over.

"I'm sure you'll hear something soon," Maggie said, as
Lydia added a splash of milk to her tea.

After voicing a doubtful hum, Lydia took a sip from
her cup. "I would like to stay and welcome him should he
show up, but I must go to the hospital today."

"And you're worried that there would be no one to
meet him at the train as he hasn't sent us a telegram."

"I am. If no one is there, he shall have to ask directions to our house. I wish I could do it, but I must check how little Ezra Baker's broken leg is mending and look in on Mrs. Carroll. She's remarkably improved, given she came in with a terrible burn to her hand." She took a big gulp of tea. "Which horse did Papa hitch to the carriage today?"

"Tybalt." Maggie recalled one of her husband's little peculiarities and smiled. "Although Papa claims to have no interest in our horses, he does seem to prefer Tybalt."

"Splendid!" Lydia got smoothly to her feet. "Romeo enjoys pulling the buggy." She planted a kiss on her mother's cheek. "I'll be back after dinner. Please don't set a place for me."

"But we shall save a *plate* for you," Maggie teased gently. "And should Captain Frost show up...?"

Lydia paused by the door and winked at Moira. "Why, give him a cup of tea, of course!"

#

Around noontime, the bell to the *Register's* door tinkled. Andy Randall looked up to find a man dressed in a Union officer's uniform: a dark blue coat, and light blue trousers with a dark blue stripe down each leg. The stranger took off his dark blue slouch hat* and stepped forward.

"Excuse me, but is Elijah Smith your editor-in-chief?"

"He is, sir," Andy replied. "I'll go fetch him for you. May I ask who is calling?"

A few minutes later, Eli energetically pegged his way into the reception room. "Captain Frost!"

The two men met in a handshake.

"What happened? We thought you'd send us a telegram telling us when you would arrive."

34

Frost smiled faintly. "The usual Army madness, I'm afraid. It took forever to process my departure from Harewood General Hospital. I had to rush to catch the train and there simply was no time to wire you. I hope Lydia isn't vexed with me."

Eli waved his concerns away. "I think she'll be delighted rather than vexed. We're about ready to close the place up for dinner. Come ride with us in the carriage. Andy and Danny can go by shank's mare."

Andy frowned. "We'll probably get there by the time everyone's finished..."

"I'll ask Mrs. Smith to make plates for you. When you arrive, you may eat your dinner in a sane manner and get back here when you can," was Eli's patient answer.

"Can we have dessert, too?" Danny blurted.

Eli sighed. "Yes, you *can* have dessert, Danny, but more importantly, you *may* have dessert."

"Thank you, Mr. Smith!"

Eli turned to Philip. "Where's your bag?"

"Left it at the depot."

"Well, go get it, man! I've got a feeling someone's waiting impatiently for you."

#

Maggie's eyes widened in surprise as Eli and the *Register* crowd surged through the door with Philip Frost in tow. Her face broke into a broad smile.

"Captain!"

He bowed. "Mrs. Smith. It's a pleasure to see you again."

Maggie curtsied as she sought the right words to cover what she feared was a breach of etiquette on her eldest daughter's part. "I'm terribly sorry, but Lydia has been called away."

It wasn't a genuine lie. Just an exaggeration of the facts. But Lydia hadn't been called away. She had made the choice to go to the hospital. *A little lie can lead to bigger things,* her conscience reminded her. It was something she used to say to Lydia and Frankie, and now repeated to Bob.

"That is," Maggie correct, "she felt she needed to leave."

"Oh. Well, where is she?"

"At the hospital."

Philip's face suddenly lit up. "I knew it! Would you be able to tell me where the hospital is?"

"It's not difficult to find," Eli replied and put a hand on the other man's shoulder, "But first, you shall dine with us. After that, I'll take you up in the carriage after I drop the others at the *Register.*"

#

"Mrs. Pearson is doing quite well after her caesarian section," Lydia was saying to Dr. Lightner as they and the hospital's nurse stood in the hall perusing the woman's chart.

Dr. Lightner gave his protégé an approving smile. "There is no sign of infection around the incision, either. Washing our hands before surgery is a wise protocol."

"I used to wash my hands when I operated in Gettysburg. Miss Edler and I also washed when attending a birth. As a result, we had only one case of puerperal fever out of ten births. Miss Edler was quite knowledgeable about Dr. Ignaz Semmelweis' work regarding cleanliness in lying-in hospitals."

The sound of footsteps caused all three to look up.

Philip Frost was striding toward them.

"Captain..." Lydia stammered. "You're here!"

"Doctor Lape." Stopping in front of her, he bowed. "How have you been?"

She curtsied. "I'm well..." She was well but flustered. Lydia never expected that Philip would come to the hospital just to see her.

Dr. Lightner's graying mustache lifted around his smile. "Nurse Van Sleet, I believe these two doctors need to have a consultation. Shall we continue our rounds?"

The slim, brunette grinned knowingly. "Of course, Dr. Lightner."

As the two disappeared into another patient's room, Lydia slipped her arm through Philip's and led him in the opposite direction.

"What are you doing here?" she whispered.

"Looking for you. Isn't it obvious?"

"Yes, but... Philip, I have heard nothing about your arrival save your last letter. I had no idea..."

Philip laughed. "Oh, Lydia! Of course, you didn't. I got delayed leaving the hospital and arrived at the depot barely in time to catch the train."

They were in the atrium now and paused to talk further, but the construction going on across the way threatened to drown their words. Workmen were repairing the door to what had been the men's wing of the Hospital for the Insane. The door had been damaged during a riot staged by a group of patients. Fortunately, the trouble behind the riot was addressed, the poor management ousted, and Dr. Winston Stanley re-installed as Superintendent. It was then that Dr. Stanley decided to split the massive Kirkbride-style* building in two, with one side reserved for the hospital for the insane and the other for a hospital for physical maladies and injuries. Due to the damage sustained, the wing for the insane would not be re-opened for another few weeks.

The loud voices of the workmen and pounding of hammers were not conducive to a conversation, so Lydia led Philip outside, where they perched on the steps of the marble portico.

"May we start over again?" Philip asked.

"Of course."

"It's good to see you, Dr. Lape."

"It's good to see you, too, Captain Frost. But why are you here? Isn't your family anxious to see you?"

His sad smile told her the story before he began to speak. "Alas, both my parents are deceased. My sister lives in the state of New York. Albany to be exact. She is married with five children and, as you can imagine has a busy life. One of my brothers lives in Ohio and the other is in the New York Cavalry. So, while I am sure they would love to see me, and I have every intention of seeing them in the future..." He took a breath. "The truth is, Lydia, I wanted to see you. I only have a week before I must to report for duty."

Lydia swallowed. "I see."

"I hope I am not being too forward."

Lydia glanced down at her hands. "No." She looked up. "No, Dr. Frost, you are not being too forward."

He thought her eyes were beautiful. Dark brown and earnest, they were not beyond sparkling when amused or teasing. They were not sparkling now. They were earnest.

"Philip," he murmured. "Call me Philip, please. Remember we agreed to use our first names."

"Philip. Yes."

"After the war, I plan to find a position as a doctor. Once I do, I would be able to entertain the notion of settling down."

"Indeed?" Lydia's heart began to thump. It had been a while since anyone had courted her.

"I know you are a widow, Lydia, and perhaps it is too soon for you to begin to consider... I mean, that is..." He trailed off.

It was with a great deal of relief that she saw he was as nervous as she. Lydia slipped an arm through his. "Philip, in truth, I still miss Edgar, and I believe I always shall. But I feel that I now am ready to consider a courtship."

His expression – one of combined delight and love – warmed her.

What Lydia did next surprised them both. She boldly leaned over and kissed him on the lips. Then she looked into his eyes as she murmured, "I think we shall be good for each other."

"Oh, Lydia," he whispered and kissed her tenderly in return.

# Chapter 4: The Idea

**8 June 1864**

"When do you need to be at Mower?" Frankie asked Patrick. She had finished sweeping the hallway and they now were sitting on the front porch.

"I have to report Sunday at 5:00 p.m. But I just got here, Frankie. Let's not talk about that now."

"That's fair." After a pause, she said, "This afternoon I will go to the hospital to help Rev. Lowry." Frankie tilted her head. "Would you like to come with me?"

"Sure. What do you do?"

"Oh, I go from room to room and talk to the patients and pray with them. But you can't come with me for that, I'm afraid. It's private."

"What should I do while you're busy?"

"Well, the grounds around the hospital are beautiful. You could sit outside."

Patrick chuckled. "How long would I have to do that? Two, three hours?"

"Two..." Frankie blushed. "It does take a while, I'm afraid. I need to talk with Rev. Lowry when I'm finished. I need to let him know if a patient is worried or if there's a problem of some sort. Then we talk and pray about it."

"Prayer sure takes up a lot of time."

She laughed softly. "As it should, Pat."

Patrick pushed his rocking chair back and forth as he thought about it. "You're really serious. You do want to be minister."

"Yes."

They were silent for a few seconds.

"Pat?" Frankie asked.

"Yeah?"

40

"If you want, you could help Joe at the hospital. He works in the barn and sees to the garden."

"Sure." The tall, lanky young man stood up and held out his hand. "That sounds better than sitting around and doing nothing. Is Joe a nice fella?"

"Oh, he's wonderful!" Frankie took his hand and he tugged her to her feet. "You won't mind helping him, will you?"

"Nah. I'll be with you all the way up and all the way home."

Frankie smiled and gave him a peck on the cheek. "I love you so!"

He chuckled. "You'd better! Not every man thinks it's okay for his wife to be a minister."

#

Earlier in the day, Lydia and Philip had borrowed the two-wheeled buggy and driven up to the hospital. While there, they made rounds, visiting a boy with a broken leg, a girl who had had an appendectomy the day before, and – separated from the rest in a room at the end of the hall – a case of the measles.

Before they went into the quarantined room, Lydia stopped Philip. "Have you had the measles?"

"Of course," he said. "You?"

"Oh, yes." She smiled at a memory. "I'm afraid I gave them to Frankie and Gideon."

Philip tilted his head. "Gideon?"

Lydia realized he did not know the details of her childhood. "He was my younger brother. Sadly, he died two years after from rheumatic fever, as did my father."

"I'm sorry, Lydia."

"It was a difficult time. I admire Mama so. Do you know she started the boarding house to provide for us?

41

She raised us all by herself, practically. I don't know how she did it."

He smiled. "I think you take after her."

"Do you? I would be honored if I were just like her." Lydia indicated the door. "Shall we visit our patient? She's eight years old and her name is Cassie. Her mother is with her."

#

After helping Joe hoe the flower beds around the cottages behind the hospital, and the beds at the front of the hospital, Patrick retired to the inviting shade of a tree.

The sun had been strong, and he was happy to be sheltered in the cool shadow made by the leaves. Settling down, Patrick planned to keep watch on the building and for Frankie.

But he promptly fell asleep instead.

He was awakened a short while later by a male voice saying, "Well, will you look who it is!"

Lydia's voice spoke next. "Frankie told us you'd be outside."

Patrick sat up as Lydia and Philip walked hand in hand toward him.

"Have a good nap?" Philip asked.

"I needed it, after helping Joe shovel out the barn." Patrick hopped to his feet. "Are you two out for a walk?"

"Actually, I'm finished for the day." Lydia stepped into the shade of the old oak. "Dr. Lightner and the nurses have given me a shorter schedule until Philip leaves for Mower."

"And I'm trying to convince her to travel with me to Philadelphia," Philip said. "It would be fun if we could explore the city before I need to report."

42

Lydia said, "I'm afraid we would need a chaperone, Philip. Even though I've been married, there is such a thing as convention."

"More's the pity," Philip joked.

"Don't let Eli hear you say that," Patrick teased. "But going to Philadelphia is a grand idea, provided we asked someone to be our escort."

Philip and Lydia sat down under the tree. All three were silent for a moment.

Philip took a breath. "Well, first of all, I'm certain we shouldn't ask Eli."

"Goodness, no!" Lydia plucked a blade of grass and chewed thoughtfully on it. "He is too protective by far. And Mama can't come because of baby Faith."

"And Emily's with child," Patrick added.

"And Grandpa might not have the stamina." Lydia heaved a sigh. "Oh, dear! I'm afraid we're running out of options."

There another silence.

Suddenly Patrick's blue eyes widened. "Wait a minute! What about Mr. Carson?"

Philip asked, "Is he a respectable man?"

"Respectable and at all times proper," Lydia replied. Her eyes grew wide with excitement. "Mr. Carson has connections with an art gallery that exhibits his photographs. He goes to visit it now and then, and he knows Philadelphia well. Let's do it! Let's ask him after supper tonight."

#

"So, would you?" Frankie asked. "Please, Mr. Carson? We can't ask Papa."

Carson smiled faintly. "I understand your hesitance. He can be rather annoying."

43

"Thank heaven someone finally had the courage to say that!"

Lydia attempted to shush her sister.

"No, Liddy," Frankie protested. "You know how Papa is, especially when he gets protective."

"Well, we needn't say such things outright. It's not polite."

Frankie turned to Patrick. "I don't think Papa has ever worried about being polite. Why should we?"

Patrick gave her shoulder an affectionate push. "Because your mother taught you not to be rude."

Frankie rolled her eyes.

Carson considered the idea as he lit his pipe. "You know..." He puffed a few smoke circles into the air. "I've been wanting to visit the Sanitary Fair. It opened yesterday and would make a splendid outing for you." With a smile, he added, "I would be delighted to be your chaperone."

#

Right before supper, Frankie, Lydia, and Carson corralled Maggie and Eli by the old stone fireplace in the kitchen's sitting area.

Frankie took the job of being the group's spokeswoman. "Mama, Papa... Liddy and I would like to accompany Patrick and Philip to Philadelphia when they report for duty."

Eli opened his mouth, but Maggie gently laid a hand on his arm. "Tell us more, dear."

Lydia said, "We know that we must have a chaperone. We have asked Mr. Carson to accompany us."

"And I accepted," Carson said. "Not only will I be their chaperone, but their tour guide, as well. I plan to show them the city of Philadelphia, as well as the Great Central Fair. It is my intent that they have some

enjoyment before our young men go to their next post."
He gave Eli a pointed look. "And, just so I do not waste
my time, I shall write a review of the fair for the *Register*."

"That's fair," Eli punned.

Frankie's face was full of hope and expectation. "We
plan to leave on Friday and spend two nights in the city."

Eli frowned. "Overnight? Where?"

"It happens I know of a hotel. It's called the Franklin
Hotel and is both suitable and kind to our pocketbooks.
I've stayed there myself and found it clean, comfortable,
and respectable."

Eli glanced at Maggie She gave him a nod.

"Well," he allowed, "the plan seems sound."

"And so, you may go," Maggie finished.

No sooner had the words left her mother's mouth
than Frankie flew into her arms.

Gathering her daughter up in a warm hug, Maggie
whispered, "Oh, dear me… Going off to Philadelphia! You
have become young women. My little girls are no more."

She reached out for Lydia and brought her oldest into
her embrace, too, as she added, "And it happened right
under my nose!" Then she kissed them each on the
cheek. "I am so very proud of you! And of your young
men."

Maggie released her daughters and wiped her eyes
with the back of her hand. Eli obligingly fished a
handkerchief from his pocket and passed it to her.

Maggie dabbed her cheeks. "Well, then, the matter is
settled. You're going to Philadelphia."

#

## 10 June 1864

Patrick and Philip had their haversacks packed and
ready to go at 6:00 a.m. Their young ladies, however,

45

needed a bit more time. Even though it was 7:00, they still had not come downstairs.

"Think we'll make the ten o'clock train?" Patrick joked over a cup of tea.

Moira, scrambling eggs at the stove, chuckled. "Now, now, Sergeant, they have a good deal more to organize than either of you."

Maggie placed a bowl of biscuits and a jar of honey before them. Patrick eagerly reached for a biscuit, as Philip asked, "Have you been to Philadelphia, Mrs. Smith?"

"Never. But I'd love to go some day."

"You should ask Mr. Smith to take you."

"I shall, but I think it would be prudent to wait until Faith is a bit older." Maggie went to the stove and ladled tapioca gruel into a small bowl. "Infants sleep a great deal; but once they start crawling..." She laughed softly. "Well, it's all any of us can do to make sure Faith doesn't get herself into trouble."

Moira added, "'Tis true, Mrs. Smith. Faith is very busy. Was Frankie like that as a babe?"

Maggie set the bowl of gruel aside to cool. "Indeed, she was!" She picked up plates of scrambled eggs and ham and brought them to the table. "She nearly ran me ragged."

Footsteps and voices sounded in the hall from the new wing, announcing the arrival of Carson, Grandpa, Nate, Eli, Edward, and the little boys. They poured into the kitchen and promptly joined the soldiers at the table.

"Say, Bob, look," Eli exclaimed. "We're having ham today! Your favorite."

"Mm," the boy agreed.

Carrying the bowl of tapioca gruel in one hand, Maggie sat down next the high chair holding her daughter. Faith reacted to the arrival of her breakfast with the baby version of excitement, waving her arms and grunting.

"I'm glad you're ready to eat, little one." Maggie dipped a small spoon into the bowl, blew on it, and offered the spoon to Faith who happily opened her mouth.

"That's my daughter," Eli bragged as he tucked a napkin into Bob's shirt. "She's got a good appetite."

Carson observed the infant, who after two spoonsful had managed to spread gruel all around her mouth. He smiled wryly. "She has similar manners, too."

The other men guffawed.

"Ha-ha," Eli grunted, taking his napkin out of its ring and spreading it over his lap. "Your attempt at humor is weak."

"But it speaks the truth."

"Are they always like this?" Philip whispered to Patrick.

Patrick nodded. "Yep."

"Where's Emily?" Maggie asked Nate. "Is she well?"

"As well as can be," the tall, dark man said. "It's difficult for her to get a good night's sleep these days."

"I remember those nights well." She used the spoon to clean gruel from around Faith's mouth. "I'll check on her as soon as the baby has eaten. I suspect she might enjoy having breakfast on a tray."

There was a clatter on the winder stairs and Frankie and Lydia, accompanied by Birgit, burst into the kitchen.

"Good morning!" Frankie chirped, plopping onto the seat beside her beau.

"About time," Patrick teased.

She punched him lightly on the arm. "Pass the eggs, please."

Lydia settled beside Philip. "I'm not used to packing for a trip. I hope I brought the proper attire."

47

"No need to worry, dear girl," Carson told her. "We will not be doing anything of a formal nature."

"They'll look beautiful no matter where you go. I saw to that," Birgit assured the young men. "Moira, is it help you're needing?"

"No," her sister replied. "Just finishing the griddle cakes. Sit and eat."

Maggie couldn't help but smile as she fed the baby another spoonful of gruel. She was happy to have a table full of cheerful, noisy conversation.

Things had been different almost a year ago when they lived in Gettysburg. Eli, Nate, and Patrick were in the field. Maggie had insisted that Nate, the little boys, Matilda and her daughter Chloe, and Grandpa move to Eli's sister and brother-in-law's farm north of the town because they anticipated a Confederate invasion.

Although Maggie was pregnant with Faith at the time, she was determined to stay in the house with Frankie and Lydia. She was taken by surprise when Emily refused to follow the others to safety. She and Maggie worked out a plan to hide her from the Confederate soldiers when they arrived. Their plan did not work out well, but somehow Maggie had convinced their invaders not to send Emily South into slavery.

As Maggie swirled the spoon through the dish of tapioca, she prayed. *Thank you for what we have today. I know others are not so fortunate, dear Lord. Help me be a light to those who need encouragement and help. May all of us here be such a light.*

#

A few hours later, Maggie, Eli, and the travelers were standing at the Blaineton depot, where they watched passengers get off the train and receive greetings from those waiting on the platform.

48

Turning, Lydia hugged her mother around the baby and whispered, "I'll miss you, Mama."

Maggie nodded as she tried not to cry.

Lydia turned to Eli next, while Frankie kissed Maggie's cheek and gave her a warm hug. "Don't worry, Mama. All will be well."

Maggie managed a brave smile. "Of course, it will."

The conductor called, "All aboard!"

The excited grins on her daughters' faces and the way their beaus escorted them to the car caused a rush of mixed feelings in Maggie's soul: joy, hope, loss... And it was almost more than she could bear.

As the two young women boarded the train, she turned to Carson. "Please keep them safe."

"I shall, my dear. You have nothing to fear." Carson surprised Maggie by giving her a kiss on the cheek.

Eli rolled his eyes. "Oh, stop being gallant, Carson, and get on the dang train."

Smiling, Carson climbed the steps to the car and disappeared inside.

Frankie leaned out a window and waved her handkerchief at Maggie and her stepfather.

"Have a good time," Maggie called.

"I will!"

"Be careful," her stepfather warned.

"I will, Papa!" She wanted to laugh at his concern. She was eighteen, for heaven's sake and off to visit Philadelphia with her beau, her sister and her beau, and their chaperone. There was no way she could not "be careful."

Lydia appeared at the window beside her sister and waved her handkerchief in farewell.

"I love you, Liddy," Maggie called.

"I love you, too, Mama! We'll see you in a few days."

The conductors signaled the all clear and the train began to chug away with a display of smoke and hiss of steam.

Maggie and Eli watched it crawl out of the station, as Maggie's eyes filled again. She cuddled Faith for comfort. "Where has the time gone, Eli? I remember when both my girls were wearing little white dresses and bonnets just like our Fay."

She was surprised to find that her husband had tears in his eyes, too.

Eli tried to sniff them back in and said, "You know, I've known Liddy since she was thirteen, and Frankie since she was a tyke of eight. Fay and Bobby are going to grow up in the blink of an eye, too, aren't they?"

"I'm afraid so. But," Maggie took a breath and straightened her spine, "we can take comfort that we are raising them the best we can. And with God's help, they will be fine young people, just like my girls."

Maggie always referred to Lydia and Frankie as "her" girls, but in a sense, they were "his" girls, too. After all, Eli had watched them grow up, too. And he had to accept the growing up and let the little girls be memories.

"Answer me one more question, sweetheart," he said.

"Of course, if I can."

"I'm only forty-four years of age. Why is it I feel sixty-five?"

A small smile came to Maggie. "Because my girls have beaus, and soon will become brides. And once they are married most likely grandchildren will start arriving."

Eli pursed his lips. "And having grandchildren puts me on a par with Grandpa O'Reilly."

Maggie laughed. "Would that be so terrible? We both would be lucky to have his energy at seventy-two."

Heaving a sigh, Eli put an arm around her shoulders. "If I'm so lucky to live that long."

She gave him a peck on the cheek to allay his fears. "The train is out of sight, my love. It's time for us to go home."

Inside the car, Frankie watched her mother and stepfather disappear and then plopped down on the seat beside Patrick. She smiled widely at him.

He grinned in return, took her hand, and settled in, relaxed and contented.

This gave Frankie the opportunity to consider a few things. Patrick and Philip Frost probably would be at the hospital until the end of the war, or until their enlistment was up. And, yet, the notion now gave Frankie a sense of peace that she had not had for nearly two years, ever since Patrick had enlisted in the army. They would be helping those wounded in the war, but safely out of the way of the bullets and the shells.

Full of hope, Frankie rested her head back against the seat and let herself be rocked by the train's motion.

# Chapter 5: Love

Frankie had been to Philadelphia in 1863. She had traveled there to fetch Patrick, who had been wounded and was recovering in Mower General Hospital. He had been shot in the leg by a nervous Union private on picket duty.

The bullet had lodged in a fleshy part of Patrick's thigh and required surgery to remove. The good news was that Patrick was well enough to be cleared to return with Frankie to Middletown, Pennsylvania.

The city had taken her breath away nearly a year ago and now, as they stepped off the train and emerged into the sunshine, Frankie gasped at the buildings and the bustle once again.

Carson shepherded the group through the streets to a horse trolley stop.

As they waited, Frankie noted that there were rails in the road. "Does a train run through here?"

Carson saw that she was pointing at the tracks. "No, my dear. That's for the horse trolley."

"It rides on a rail?"

"Yes."

"Why doesn't it have an engine?"

With an indulgent smile, Carson said, "Because a great steam engine belching smoke would be quite inconvenient on a city street, wouldn't it?"

In a short while, Frankie caught sight of the horse trolley. Indeed, a team of two horses were pulling what appeared to be a smaller version of a railroad car. Excited about this new experience, she waited as the vehicle pulled up beside them.

From what she could see, the car was full of people, but at Carson's instructions, she fished the correct amount of change from her purse, and paid the conductor standing at the rear of the vehicle.

"I'll take your bag, miss," the conductor said, wrenching it from her hand and tossing it into a small compartment just inside.

"Thank you," she stammered, and followed Carson into the car.

Frankie was surprised to see that, rather than having seats arranged horizontally, the interior of the car had two long benches arranged vertically with an aisle in the middle. Riders sat facing the aisle with their backs to the windows. There were eight windows on either side of the car, indicating that the designer had intended for eight passengers on either side.

As far as Frankie could tell there were ten or twelve on either side with more people squashed in the aisle.

As the trolley began to move, she briefly lost her balance and collided with Carson, who looked over his shoulder. "Are you all right, my dear?"

"I'm fine, Mr. Carson."

There were so many people on board that the pressure of being squashed between Carson and Patrick held Frankie fast, which was a good thing, as there was nothing for her to hold on to. She couldn't see a thing for all the bodies and wondered how anyone would know when to get off and how they would get out once they arrived at their stop. Surely, people would climb over her.

"Do you see Liddy?" she asked.

"Yeah," Patrick said. "Looks like she got a seat."

"Of course, she did..." Frankie pouted. Lydia was tall and beautiful, and it would be natural for a gentleman to give up his seat for her. She, on the other hand, was short and red-haired, and was wondering if people believed her to be an Irish maid and therefore didn't deserve a seat. *That's unfair*, she thought. *Just because someone's a maid doesn't mean her feet aren't tired.*

53

After a sweaty 45 minutes of traveling, stopping, having passengers pressing past her and shoving her nearly onto the laps of seated people, Frankie heard Carson finally cry, "Ah, our stop! To the door, Patrick!"

As the wagon halted, Frankie followed in Patrick's wake as it was their turn to shove their way to the exit.

When they alighted on a cobbled street. Frankie gratefully took a breath of the remarkably cooler air, even though it was filled with the odor of horse manure, human sweat, and smoke. It was, in fact, not all that different from Blaineton proper's air, save more intense.

"Look out, miss!"

She just barely avoided being struck by her carpet bag as it came flying out of the trolley.

"Well," she huffed, "I don't believe the conductor would have been concerned in the least had he hit me." Picking up her bag, she turned to her companions.

Before Frankie could completely collect herself, Carson gestured that they walk up the street, and off they went.

A ten-minute hike later, they were standing before the Franklin Hotel. Located on North 3rd Street, it was just one street below Race Street and catered to people and families of the middling classes.

As Frankie gazed at the three-story building's façade, she realized that she had never been in a hotel before. The lobby, unlike the streets was hushed. It was decorated with chairs and sofas covered in maroon velvet and wooden straight-back chairs with floral designs embroidered on their cushions. The entrance was at one end of the lobby and the registration desk – a long, ornately carved affair – was at the other.

Carson strode to desk, the rest of the party trailing behind him.

Frankie whispered to Lydia as they watched him sign in. "How did he know they'd have room?"

"He wired them," was the reply.

"You can do that?"

"Evidently."

Carson turned to them. "It is as I stated, the cost is one dollar and fifty cents a night. That includes meals."

The young people opened their purses and gave him three dollars each, which he turned over to the man behind the counter.

"We are in luck," Carson said as they picked up their bags, "they had three rooms available on the third floor. Two are side by side and the other is across the hall."

When Frankie and Lydia entered their room, Frankie gasped and said, "Ohh, look, Liddy!"

The room was tidy and smelled clean. It contained two beds, a wardrobe, a washstand with basin, pitcher, soap, and towels, and a small bureau. The window was graced with dark blue draperies with a lace curtain behind.

Frankie threw herself on the bed nearest the window. "It's so beautiful and comfortable!"

Lydia laughed and fell onto the bed nearest the door. "Yes! It's heavenly!"

Frankie sat up, drew back the lace curtains and gazed out the window. To Maggie's daughters, they had just walked into a new world. Frankie dropped the curtain and chirped, "We're in a city! There are tall buildings! And just listen to the wagons and the people on the street! It's wonderfully noisy."

"And it'll probably keep us up all night," Lydia teased.

"Not I! I shall probably fall asleep from sheer exhaustion."

Lydia lay back with her arms behind her head. "Mr. Carson says we'll take our dinner downstairs in a real restaurant."

"Everything seems so grand, Liddy. Do you think our clothing will be acceptable?"

"We brought our Sunday best," was Lydia's common-sense reply. "Our clothing is clean, and it isn't worn. We shall be proud of who we are and what we are wearing."

#

The hotel's restaurant was not grand, as Frankie had feared, but it was attractive and respectable. White table cloths and vases of flowers were on the tables and there were men wearing white jackets and black trousers to take their orders.

To accompany the meal, Carson, Philip, and Patrick ordered red wine, while the girls, raised by teetotaler Maggie, chose to drink tea.

Eventually, Frankie gathered enough courage to take a sip from Patrick's glass, but immediately made a face. "It's sour. I don't like it."

"Your Mama would be so proud," Patrick teased.

The five enjoyed a four-course meal: vegetable soup with macaroni, a salad of greens with a mayonnaise dressing, and roasted chicken and gravy with potatoes and peas. The fourth course, the dessert, was vanilla ice cream covered with fresh strawberries and a strawberry sauce.

"I understand the chef at Blaineton's new hotel plans to offer ice cream," Frankie said as her dessert was placed before her. "I've never had it before." She picked up her spoon and poked at the frozen treat.

Lydia took a bite. As soon as the concoction hit her tongue, she closed her eyes and sighed. "Oh... this is lovely! Gentlemen you may keep your wine."

"I'll see that you get ice cream every day while we're here," Philip told her.

She grinned at him. "Would you? That is quite gallant of you."

"You deserve to be happy."

Frankie, now tucking happily into her dish of ice cream, joked, "She must have her 'just deserts': she deserves dessert."

They all groaned at her bad pun.

#

After dinner, Carson took them to the art gallery where his photographs were displayed. The respectful hush within the building impressed the young people, who were amazed to see photographs framed and hanging on the wall like paintings.

"It's almost like art," Frankie whispered.

"It *is* art," Carson corrected.

"Which ones are yours, Mr. Carson?" Lydia asked.

"Come with me." The silver-haired man led them to a section displaying a series of photographs he had taken while traveling with Eli as a war correspondent, as well as a set taken at Gettysburg after the battle.

"Oh, my goodness," Lydia exclaimed. "Frankie, look! It's Papa."

The others joined her by a photograph of Eli taking a nap next to his news wagon. He was lying upon the ground, with his arms behind his head, supporting it like a pillow. His hair was long and shaggy, his beard scruffy and uneven. Eli's eyes were shut and his mouth slightly open.

Frankie giggled. "He looks like a beggar!"

"That sure brings back memories." Patrick glanced at Carson. "Eli was snoring, wasn't he?"

Smiling affectionately, Carson nodded.

"Carson? Could it be? Why it *is* you! Chester Carson, you old dog!"

The quintet turned as a smiling brown-haired man of medium height strode them.

"Alfred Benning! Good to see you again, old chap."

Carson met his friend in a firm, friendly handshake.

"What the deuce brings you to my gallery without your telling me? Shame on you!"

Carson stepped back and indicated his four companions. "It was a last-minute plan. These two young men are Captain Philip Frost and Sergeant Patrick McCoy. They are to report for duty at Mower General Hospital on Sunday morning." The two soldiers bowed. "And these two lovely young ladies are Mrs. Lydia Lape and Miss Frances Blaine."

Frankie and Lydia dropped curtsies.

"Ladies and gentlemen, may I introduce my friend Alfred T. Benning, owner of the Philadelphia Gallery of Photographic Art."

Benning aimed an exaggerated bow in their direction. "Your servant, good people. What may I do for you good people?"

"We are seeing the sights," Carson said. "Have you any recommendations regarding what we might do this evening?"

"When do I not? In fact, I happen to know of a concert of sacred music being held at a church not far from here. It begins at 7:00 o'clock and all you need do is put an offering in the plate."

Frankie's face lit up. "Will they have a real orchestra?"

"Of course."

"Oh, Mr. Carson, may we?" She slipped her arm through his. "I'm sure Mama would approve."

He patted the back of her hand. "I'm sure she would, my dear. And go, we shall. That is, if the rest of you would like to hear the concert."

The others readily agreed.

Carson turned to his friend. "Well, then, Benning, we are in your hands. What time would you like to meet us here?"

"Let us say 6:00 o'clock. We shall enjoy the concert and for support repair to an excellent little oyster house I know. The meal will be my gift to you."

"You needn't do that," Carson said.

"I needn't, but I wish to. My dear chap, I am delighted to see you and meet these lovely young people." He fished a pocket watch out of his waistcoat and consulted it. "Ah! I'm afraid I must greet a gentleman in a few minutes. He wishes to look at my collection. With any luck, he'll purchase something. Until 6:00 o'clock, dear friends."

#

The afternoon was a whirlwind of activity as Carson took the young people all over Philadelphia. They visited the Pennsylvania State House and stared up at the steeple that housed the Liberty Bell.

Frankie couldn't believe she was walking where Benjamin Franklin and many of the other Founders of her nation had walked. And notion of the Liberty Bell, named by the abolition movement in the 1830s, warmed her heart. Like her mother, she believed that all people were equal and should be free.

Later they toured the Academy of Natural Sciences of Philadelphia and took in the art at the Philadelphia Academy of the Fine Arts. Lydia found the collections in the Academy of Natural Sciences fascinating, while Frankie was moved by the paintings and sculptures at the fine arts academy. Frankie's world, previously bounded by her experiences in Blaineton and more recently in Gettysburg, expanded and exploded with a palpable bang.

Lydia, meanwhile, found her mind expanded by the exhibits, and was not immune from the power of the city's culture and history as she walked arm in arm with

Philip. She was exhilarated by the city and by the things it had to offer.

But what made it all the sweeter was being with Philip. It reminded her of how it had been with Edgar. They had shared life in her mother's boarding house. Only that morning she had dreamed of Edgar. She remembered how he had smiled at her and said, "You need a partner, Liddy. Don't be afraid. If you hesitate, you may never have another chance."

As Lydia had packed that morning she asked herself a thousand questions and tried to understand the short, but powerful vision. She wondered if perhaps her mind was giving her permission to have feelings for another man. Surely, she did have feelings for Philip. They were growing by the moment.

Before she had learned of Edgar's death, she had experienced a dream, too. In that one, her husband had said, "I'm all right, Liddy. Don't be afraid." That and the more recent memorable dream caused her to wonder if it was possible for the dead to communicate with the living. It certainly seemed so.

Yet, another part of her said perhaps she just needed to do what she thought was best. It was, after all, her life.

By the end of their tour, both Lydia's mind and feet were tired. Fortunately, they had time to retire to a park where they sat on the benches to rest before they left to meet Mr. Benning.

Lydia and Philip took a bench all to themselves, while Carson, good chaperone that he was, opted to sit with Frankie and Patrick.

"What do you think of Philadelphia?" Philip asked.

"It's lovely. And so exciting." As she glanced at him, she decided to be bold. "And I'm glad I'm sharing it with you."

Philip's hand closed over hers.

It pleased her the way his hand comfortably enveloped hers. It made her feel safe and at ease. She hadn't felt that way in a long time. Content, Lydia surrendered and rested her head on his shoulder.

Her response was natural and open – and Philip wanted to kiss her. Such a thing, though, would be improper in a public place. So, he decided to talk instead. "Liddy, if you don't mind my asking, what was Edgar like?"

Lydia sighed softly. "Edgar was a fine man, Phil. He was a lawyer and oh, so intelligent, perhaps even brilliant. He was of course serious, but not so serious as not to know how to laugh and have fun." Despite her best efforts, she sighed again.

"I'm sorry, Lydia. This war is so cruel."

"It is," she agreed. "Too many women have found themselves in my position." She lifted her head and gazed into his eyes. "I feel very lucky now."

"Do you?"

"Yes. I have found someone different from Edgar and yet as compatible with me as Edgar had been."

That made his heart soar. "Oh, my dear, Lydia. Thank you. I had hoped..."

"What had you hoped?"

He gathered his nerve and finished, "That you might feel that way."

"What about you, Phil? Did you have someone? A girl? Or a wife perhaps?"

Philips eyes followed a family as it passed them. It was comprised of a father, mother, and two little children whom he judged to be two and four years of age. The couple seemed to share a beautiful intimacy. They spoke quietly to each other as they held the hand of a rambunctious child chafing to run on the grass. He longed for a family like that.

"I was interested in a girl or two," Philip replied. "But I never married." He met her eyes. "However, I should like to share my life, but not just with anyone. I've always had a dream that the woman I marry would be my partner in the truest sense of the word."

Emboldened further, Lydia replied, "Then you would have no objection if that woman were a physician?"

"My dear, Lydia, I would be honored to have such a woman by my side."

She wasn't one who blushed easily, but she did. Casting her eyes shyly downward, she said, "And I would be honored to have a man with those sentiments by mine."

"Would you? Would you be honored indeed?"

When Lydia lifted her head and gazed at him, Philip thought she was the most beautiful woman he had ever met. And Lydia was finding him to be the intelligent, caring man she had hoped to meet in due time. What surprised her was that "due time" had come so quickly.

"Answer me, Lydia," Philip persisted, "would you truly be honored to have such a man by your side?"

"Yes," she replied. "Yes, I would, because that man is you."

"Oh, my dear..." Impulsively, he lifted her hand and kissed the back of it. When he glanced up, he noticed that their friends across the way had seen his indiscretion. Frankie was giggling, and Patrick and Carson were nudging each other.

Philip quickly released Lydia's hand.

"We are being watched," he whispered. "I'm afraid we're making a spectacle of ourselves."

Lydia returned her hand to her lap, but chuckled. "Yes, and I'm sure we'll be teased about it, too. But do you know what, Phil?

"What?"

"I don't care."

"Neither do I." He gathered his nerve once again. "Lydia?"

She brought her questioning eyes up to meet his.

"Would you do me the honor of becoming my wife?"

There was a quick intake of breath, followed by, "Yes. Oh, yes, Phil, I would be honored and happy to be your wife."

After an awkward pause on his part, Philip cleared his throat. "I would love to kiss you right now, my dear, but..." He nodded in the direction of the trio on the other park bench.

Lydia's smile rewarded him, as did her next words. "Don't worry, my love. You may kiss me later."

#

The small group soon returned to the photography gallery, where they met Alfred Benning and followed his lead to the Episcopal church, where the concert was to be held.

As Frankie stepped into the sanctuary, her mouth dropped open. She had never seen a church so grand, yet so unassuming. Simple white paint adorned its walls. Graceful pillars supported its ceiling. And the aisle, flanked by white pews with dark brown trim, led to an arch under which the altar and an old-fashioned raised pulpit sat. All of this was dominated by the tall window of clear glass panes behind it.

Frankie still was gaping when Benning said, "This way, please. I think you will enjoy sitting in the balcony. The organ is up there, and it is magnificent."

She and the others followed the gallery owner up a set of narrow stairs. And then Frankie gaped more, for the view from the balcony took her breath away.

"Oh, and look," she whispered to Patrick as she pointed discreetly. "I've never seen organ pipes this grand. The Presbyterian church in Blaineton has a pipe organ, but it's nothing like this. This must shake the rafters!"

Shortly after they were seated, a small orchestra and the choir processed in and arranged themselves on seats in the apse.

Frankie glanced at her program. The first piece they would hear was Bach's Cantata BVW 140, "Wake up, the voice calls us."

If there is a voice within music, it did indeed call. For once the piece began, Frankie felt her soul swept away by it. Thrilled, she followed the translation of the German words listed in the program as the sound of the instruments and the voices swirled around her.

*This must be what heaven is like*, she thought.

She was especially moved by the soprano and bass aria. It was a conversation between Jesus and the Soul. Her heart grew warm when the Soul sang, "Come, Jesus!" and Jesus answered, "Come, lovely soul!"

*Oh, yes*, she thought. The conversation was a call that she needed to – no, that she would – answer. She had no idea where it would lead but believed with her whole heart that the call came from God.

Lydia was seated beside Frankie but was having a different response to the music. It stirred up gratitude in her because she had been fortunate to find someone with whom she could work and live and love. She had found it first with Edgar. Now she had been blessed again to find it with Philip.

She thought: *I almost let Philip go by. Thank you, God, for giving him the patience to wait until I was ready.*

She glanced at the man sitting beside her and smiled.

Philip turned his head and returned the smile. Then he leaned close, whispering in her ear, "This would be a lovely place to get married, don't you think?"

"It would indeed," she whispered back.

Their eyes met again.
And their smiles broadened.

#

Frankie wrinkled her nose as the waiter placed a bowl of a brown gravy-like soup before Carson and Benning. "What's in snapper soup?"

Carson dipped his spoon into the bowl. "Snapping turtle, my dear, among other things."

At this, the young woman drew back. "Turtle? In the soup? The whole thing? Shell and all?"

Benning chuckled. "No. It's turtle meat with onions, carrots, and celery."

"And garlic," Carson added.

"Yes. It's savory and altogether delightful! A Delaware Valley specialty."

Frankie shuddered as she queasily watched the two men savor their soup. "I had a pet turtle once," she said. "When it died, we buried it. I don't think I could have eaten it. I'm glad I ordered the clam chowder and fried haddock." She picked up the soup spoon and sampled her appetizer.

"Me, too." Patrick reached for the breadbasket sitting in the middle of the table. "It's kind of hard to have feelings for a clam."

Craning her neck, Frankie searched the room. It was crowded with diners, all consuming seafood. "I wonder what's keeping Lydia and Philip?"

Patrick liberally spread butter over a piece of bread. "Don't worry. They said they wanted to stay behind to tour the church. They probably stopped somewhere else to eat." He nudged her with his elbow. "I imagine they're looking for a little privacy."

"Not too much privacy, I hope." Frankie took a taste of her clam chowder. "They shouldn't be out without a chaperone."

The young sergeant hooted. "Darlin', your sister was a married woman!"

"Lower your voice," Frankie hissed. "Liddy's proper. She'd never do anything wanton."

"Aw, take it easy. I didn't mean she'd do anything wrong. It's just they probably need a little time alone." Patrick took a big bite of bread. "Mm. I don't get bread like this in the army." He held it out to her. "Try it."

Frankie laughed. "Now, *that* would be improper. Me eating from your hand!"

"Come on. Be improper. No one cares here."

Grinning, Frankie took a bite.

"I say," Benning commented as the main course was brought out, "I have an idea. Why don't we all go to the Great Central Fair tomorrow?"

Frankie took a taste of her haddock and then said, "We plan to, Mr. Benning. I scarce can wait. Papa wrote all about it in the *Register*."

"Correction," Carson said, "*I* wrote all about it in the *Register*. I had hoped the initial information would encourage people to attend."

"Did it work?" Frankie asked.

The older man's white mustache turned up with his smile. "I have no idea. But I intend to write a more detailed review after our visit. They have a New Jersey exhibit there, you know."

"I'm glad to hear you plan to attend," Benning said. "We'll make a day of it. It will be a splendid send off for Sergeant McCoy, and Captain Frost. And, best of all, we shall be able to donate to the Sanitary Commission."

#

66

Two hours later, the little party tumbled back into the hotel. Carson retreated to his room, leaving Frankie and Patrick in the hallway. While he took his job of chaperone seriously, Carson also understood the young couple's need for a few moments alone.

Frankie and Patrick stood hand in hand for a moment. The gas lamps flickered around them and all was quiet since most people had retired to their rooms.

Patrick looked around to ensure that they were truly alone. Then he put his arms around Frankie. "This is goodnight, honey, until tomorrow." He gave her a warm kiss.

Frankie clung to him. "I know we've got another day, Pat, but I don't want you to go to Mower."

"I don't want to go, either, but I've got a commitment to fulfill."

They held each other for a long, sweet moment.

Frankie whispered, "Someday we won't have to say goodnight and go to separate rooms."

Their next kiss was deep and loving. Frankie thought it was their best kiss so far.

Patrick grinned. "Remember that night in York?"

She giggled. "It wasn't terribly romantic, was it?"

"Well, if it had been, Eli would've had us married by now."

Frankie sighed. "You asked me then. Maybe we should have gotten married."

Patrick shook his head. "No." He tipped her chin up so he could look into her eyes. "When we finally get married, honey, we're going to do it right."

Frankie smiled. "You're a good man, Pat."

"And you're a good woman."

They kissed again, this time briefly, and drew apart. Yet, Frankie still couldn't help but reach for his hand one more time.

"Sleep well," she said.

He squeezed her hand. "You, too, dear."

Their rooms were across the hall from each other. Patrick turned to his and Frankie to hers. She had her hand on the door knob and was about to turn it, when she heard a woman scream and Patrick exclaim, "What the hell!"

She whirled around in time to see Patrick quickly pull the door shut.

"Jesus," he exclaimed.

"Patrick! Language!"

Tying the sash to his dressing gown, Carson rushed out of his room and into the hallway. "Good heavens, what is going on out here? You'll wake the dead and get us thrown out in the bargain."

Patrick mutely pointed to the door to his room.

Then the door opened and Philip, clad in his trousers and an unbuttoned shirt, slipped into the hall, carefully shutting the door behind him. He cleared his throat. "Perhaps I should explain..."

"Yeah." Patrick said. "Perhaps you should. Why is Lydia in there?"

"Lydia!?" Frankie stepped forward. "Philip! How dare you!"

Carson clasped a hand around her upper arm before she could slug the Captain. "Let the man speak, my dear."

"It's... well..." Philip took a breath. "We... ah... that is..." He took another breath and finished quickly, "Lydia and I got married."

Frankie's face went so pale, her freckles stood out like a case of the measles. "M-married?"

"Yes. After everyone left the church, we asked the rector to marry us." Seeing the skeptical expressions on the others' faces, he stammered, "I have the license if you'd like to see it. It's all perfectly legal."

Carson sighed. "There is no need to see it, Captain Frost. I believe you. But... ah..." He looked around at the others in the small group. "We obviously will need to make different sleeping arrangements."

Everyone was still for a moment.

Finally, Patrick said, "I don't suppose..."

"No," Frankie blurted before he finished the sentence.

"I didn't mean you!" He glanced at Carson. "I can't afford to rent another room. And since we have three rooms..."

Now it was Carson's turn to sigh. "You want to share my room with me."

Patrick nodded.

Carson resignedly tightened the sash to his robe. "I'll keep a lamp on for you." With that, he disappeared into his room.

There was another silence.

Finally, Frankie said, "Tell Liddy congratulations, Philip." She managed a smile. "I'm glad you're my brother-in-law. It just took me by surprise."

He chuckled. "It took me by surprise, too. I'm glad you're my sister-in-law and delighted that your sister is my wife. Good night, everyone." And with that he retreated into the room.

*

Clutching the bedsheet to her, Lydia sat up. "What did you tell them?"

"That we're married." Philip shut the door behind him.

"How did they take it?"

He removed his shirt. "There were a variety of responses."

Lydia heaved a sigh. "I don't blame them. This isn't like me at all."

Philip paused. "You don't regret it, do you, Lydia?"

Smiling, she brushed her dark hair away from her face. "No. Of course not."

"Are you sure?"

She laughed now. "For heaven's sake, Phil, get into bed so I can show you how little I regret it."

Grinning, Philip began to unbutton his trousers.

"Don't forget to bolt the door this time."

Never taking his eyes off his new wife, Philip reached behind him and pulled the bolt across, locking them out from the rest of the world.

"Now," Lydia said, lifting the sheet and affording him a fine view, "Come to bed, my love..."

#

## 11 June 1864

Shortly after dawn, Frankie heard a light rap on the door. Rubbing the sleep from her eyes, she called. "I'm coming." Throwing the covers back, she slipped out of bed, but paused when she reached the door. She was, after all, in a city. "Who is it?" she cautiously asked.

"It's Lydia! For heaven's sake, Frankie, let me in."

Frankie threw back the bolt and opened the door.

A disheveled Lydia slipped into the room. Her hair was loose, several buttons undone on her waist, her skirt appeared to be on backward, and she was carrying her shoes and stockings.

Frankie shut the door behind her and threw the bolt.

An awkward silence ensued until Lydia said, "I'm sorry. I should have told you, but we didn't know we were going to get married." She sank down onto what had once been her bed.

Frankie sat beside her sister. "Why did you do it?"

Lydia thought a moment. "Quite honestly, I don't know. We had spoken briefly about marriage in the park

70

yesterday. Phil proposed, I accepted. But while we were at the concert we suddenly didn't want to wait."

"What will Mama say?"

"Oh, I'm sure she'll be happy once she's over the surprise. But she'll be sad that we didn't plan a wedding in the usual manner. But you know Mama. She'll understand. After all, she eloped with our father."

Frankie winced. "But Papa won't understand. Not at all."

Lydia chuckled. "Not right away. But Mama will reel him in."

Frankie took her sister's hand. "I'm happy for you, Liddy, but are you done mourning for Edgar?"

"Done? No, dearest, I'll never be done mourning for Edgar." Tears came to her eyes and she brushed them away. "One doesn't ever stop mourning, I think. The pain is not as sharp as time passes, but I'm convinced it never disappears completely."

"Are you sure you love Philip?"

"Yes. Edgar and I were first loves, Frankie. It was quite intense and based on a long-term friendship. I think, in my heart, I knew that the war would take Edgar. That's why when it started I wanted to marry him. I wouldn't have wanted to wonder what our marriage would have been like, only to be left with dreams. It would have been too tragic." She squeezed Frankie's hand. "But Philip and I... well, we have passion, of course, but we also are well met intellectually and emotionally. He understands my love of medicine and my desire to help others because he feels the same things."

"What about children? How will you work when you have a baby?"

Lydia tweaked her sister's nose. "Frances! For goodness sake! Our mother kept a boarding house and raised us while she was a widow. If Phil and I have a family, we will continue our work as doctors. It will take some doing, but we will accomplish our dreams."

"You're so brave!"

"Hardly. But I'm strong and Phil knows my heart, so let the future be what it may." She brushed escaped strands of wavy red hair from her sister's face. "I believe the secret to a good marriage is mutual respect and growing knowledge of each other. I do wish, though, that Philip and I had not been so impulsive as to take the room from Patrick."

Frankie giggled. "Liddy! It was your wedding night!"

"Well, yes... but to have Patrick walk in like that... We thought you'd be back much later. I suppose time got away from us."

"Was it terribly embarrassing?"

"No! Things had not progressed very far. And Patrick didn't see into the room."

Frankie nudged her sister. "Did you like it?"

"Oh, for heaven's sake, Frances!"

"Well, did you?"

"Yes. And you will, too, when you and Patrick are wed."

"Are you sure?"

"Frankie, what goes on between men and women is natural. There's nothing wrong with it. Both man and woman ought to enjoy each other, although sometimes it takes the woman a little longer to find enjoyment. But it's actually rather simple." She patted Frankie's hand. "There! I've told you the facts, but I'm sure Mama will tell you again before you're married."

Suddenly, Frankie grimaced.

"What's wrong?"

"Eli... and Mama." She shuddered.

Lydia grabbed a pillow and swung it at her sister. "Stop it!"

72

Laughing, Frankie seized another pillow and began to pummel her sister.

# Chapter 6: The Great Central Fair

Alfred Benning joined the little group for breakfast at the hotel's restaurant and gave each person copies of the *Philadelphia Sanitary Fair Catalogue & Guide*. Frankie had her nose in the brochure throughout her eggs, sausage, and potatoes, and was still reading as she sipped her tea.

"This should be a jolly fair, according to the *Guide*," Lydia commented.

"Yes," Philip said. "But the Sanitary Commission is such a noble endeavor. It has made great strides combating illness in our camps and providing food for our soldiers and aiding the wounded. We need to contribute as generously as we are able."

Patrick agreed. "When I was laid up in Mower, a Sanitary Commission volunteer helped me send a telegram to Frankie to let her know I had been wounded and where I was."

Frankie abruptly looked up from the *Guide*. "Do you know how much money these fairs have raised? Chicago was the first one. They brought in eighty-thousand dollars. And the fair in New York City raised over *one million dollars*." She flopped back in her chair, picked up her tea cup, and took a gulp. "I'm so proud of average people like us! We can do anything when we work together."

Carson smiled at the young woman. "What would you like to see today, Frankie?"

"The Floral Department! It sounds lovely."

"Relics and Curiosities for me," Patrick piped in.

"Nor should we miss the William Penn Parlor," Carson added. "Elijah should visit it to see how his ancestors lived."

Benning chuckled. "You should have him visit the Pennsylvania Kitchen, as well. It's another re-creation of our forebears' way of life."

"We ought to go to the Art Gallery and the Photographic Gallery," Lydia commented. "I should think they both would be quite interesting."

Frankie grinned. "I bet Mr. Carson's photographs are far superior."

Carson waved her comments away, but Benning said, "I agree whole-heartedly, Miss Blaine. Our Mr. Carson is quite talented."

"Oh, now, that is too much, Benning." Carson fished his watch out of his vest pocket and checked the time. "Let's get going, shall we? As Elijah says, daylight is burning."

#

The little party left the hotel and strolled along Race Street until they came to Logan Square, where the 200,000 square-foot complex housing the Great Central Fair sat. The structure had been built by volunteer construction workers in the span of forty days. Now the flag of the United States of America flew on a 216-foot flag pole over the imposing edifice.

They stopped at the Eighteenth Street and Race Street entrance.

"I think perhaps we should split up and meet for dinner," Patrick suggested.

Frankie consulted the *Guide*. "The restaurant looks enormous. How will we find everyone?"

Lydia looked at the map over her sister's shoulder. "If we agree to meet by its Union Avenue entrance at noon, it should be fine. Shall we do that?"

"Let us," Carson said. "What does it say of the restaurant?"

Frankie turned to the appropriate page, read, and said, "It has first-class dishes, all reasonably priced. Nothing is more than 35 cents."

"Sounds good," Patrick said. "Let's meet at the restaurant entrance on Union Avenue at noon."

"Listen to what the Guide says about the building!" Before anyone could respond, Frankie enthusiastically began to read: "The building is constructed in the Gothic style, occupying the whole of Logan Square, forming two buildings taking in the gravel walks, one along Race and the other along Vine street, extending from Eighteenth to Nineteenth Streets. The main Transept runs the entire length of the Square, from east to west. From this Transept (which has been very appropriately named Union Avenue) all the other buildings branch off on both sides."*

She paused for breath.

Carson leaned toward Patrick and murmured, "Benning and I shall meet you at the Restaurant." With that the two men strolled away.

Oblivious to their defection, Frankie read on. "On the north is the Floral Department, on the south side is the Restaurant, and the Art Gallery occupies the entire length of the Vine Street end of the square. Union Avenue is five hundred feet long and sixty-four feet wide, running east and west. It is a splendid Gothic arch, and the entire length is supported by latticed ribs, which spring from the ground meeting in the center."*

Philip took Lydia's arm. "We'll see you at dinner," he told Patrick. And they, too, walked off.

That left Patrick standing with his girl, who continued to read.

"Beautiful as such an immense length of delicate lattice-worked girders naturally is, the effect is greatly heightened by the foliage of the trees having been allowed to festoon themselves within the Transept, so that standing at either end, an immense vista of gay colors present themselves, the whole being garlanded high up with our national colors of Red, White and Blue, and this again being brought into contrast with the delicate green of the foliage of the trees; indeed the whole conveys such a Kaleidoscopic picture, that when once seen can scarce ever be driven from the retina – "*

"For heaven's sake, Frankie," her frustrated beau interrupted. "Are we gonna stand here all day while you read to me, or are we gonna go inside and see this thing?"

"Oh," she said. "We'll see it, certainly." She looked up., "Where did everyone go?"

Patrick rolled his eyes.

#

"Oh, look," Lydia exclaimed as they entered the first hall after Philip had paid their entrance fee. "It's the Delaware Department!"

Philip consulted the *Guide*. "The New Jersey Department is this way."

They toured the display of battle flags, cannons, and swords from New Jersey's part in the war and from the state's history. Once the couple had perused everything, they sauntered back up the "street" and turned onto Union Avenue.

Lydia gasped out loud. "Oh, my! Will you look?"

The hall stretched over 540 feet in length. Tables filled with exhibits lined both walls and the center of the avenue. Gothic arches stretched overhead, as well as a profusion of flags in a colorful display of red, white, and blue.

"What a sight to see!"

"Amazing," Philip said. "I can't wait to see the rest of it. Shall we go to the Floral Department?"

"I'd love to. Where is it?"

He checked his *Guide.* "Just past the Arms and Trophies Department."

Lydia laughed. "And where, pray tell, is that?"

Philip pointed straight ahead. "Shall we?"

When they entered the Floral Department, Lydia's breath was taken away once more. The explosion of green plants and rainbow of flowers was unlike any she had ever seen. And the large fish pond with a fountain in its center entranced her.

"It's all so beautiful," she murmured.

Philip leaned close and whispered in her ear, "You are more beautiful."

She favored him with a smile.

"Stay here for a moment, please. I'll be back shortly."

Although she mildly wondered where her new husband had gone, Lydia was content to stand and watch the fish swimming in the pond while the water played in the fountain.

Philip returned fifteen minutes later, grinning ear to ear and keeping one hand behind his back.

"Welcome back," she said. "Where did you go? And what are you hiding?"

Grinning, he brought his right hand around to present her with a bouquet of roses.

Lydia took the bunch and inhaled their fragrance. "Oh, they're lovely, Philip!"

"Well, you're my bride and I realized that brides should have flowers. I didn't want you to do without."

"You're a dear." She checked to see if anyone was watching – they weren't - and gave him a quick peck on the cheek.

"You're my rose, Liddy. More beautiful than these by half."

His words made her blush and it took her a moment to speak. "Well, Philip, if I may be so bold, I never thought I would be so happy again."

"Do you know what I think?"

"What?"

"I think we both are fortunate that God brought us together and that we were wise enough to notice."

Lydia looped her arm through his and rested her head on his shoulder. "May we stand here a bit longer and watch the waters?"

"I can think of nothing better, my love."

#

The Art Gallery was located directly behind the Floral Department. Here the walls were packed with paintings and drawings, while sculptures were displayed on tables and in cabinets.

Carson and Benning soon found the photography section and walked slowly along discussing the merits of the new technology.

"No matter what others say, it *is* art, the same as painting or drawing," Benning murmured. "It's a composition that communicates an idea, a moment, a person..."

Carson nodded.

"But, frankly, dear friend, your work is far superior to this."

"Thank you."

Benning cleared his throat and in a lowered voice said, "I know we have spoken of this before, but should you ever decide to leave Blaineton –"

"Ah," Carson interrupted. "Yes. The question."

"If you were to move here, I could arrange things, so you would give lectures and have shows in places other than my gallery."

79

"In exchange for what?"

Benning frowned. "Chester! In exchange for nothing. I think we share the same feelings, do we not?"

Carson took a deep breath as he pretended to study a photograph of several soldiers grouped around a tent. "Yes. Yes, we do. But here is my dilemma, dear chap. I clearly understand that photography could be, and perhaps will be, my second chance, my second career, as it were. However, I must ask whether one gets a second chance in other areas of one's life." He lifted his eyes now to meet Benning's. "Perhaps the answer to that is not as important as my own answer, which is I don't want a second chance."

Benning's expression was let down, but he said, "Was he that precious?"

"He was everything. Why would I want more?"

"And your Mr. Smith?"

Carson chuckled. "A brother only. God save me, if it were something else. Besides, that is not his way. He's well matched with Mrs. Smith. Yet, if I were to leave him, I would need to be assured that he will make good of his present situation. I'm sure he can do it. He is proving himself every day."

There was a pause as Carson considered something else.

"And then there's Mrs. Smith – Maggie. Benning, she took me in when I had next to nothing. She has loved me with purity and honesty, despite my low estate. Life without her... and without the others in the house... well, I'm afraid I would feel terribly lonely."

Benning clapped Carson on the arm. "Good God, man, do you know what you are describing?"

Carson blinked at him.

"A family! They're your family!"

"So, they are," he murmured, slightly surprised. He returned his gaze to Benning. "Under those circumstances, then, why would I leave?"

"I am disappointed, of course, but I understand. In fact, I am envious." Benning gazed at the photograph again. "Carson, did you know that this was taken at Antietam?"

"Was it? Smith and I wandered into the aftermath. It was a dreadful situation. Whoever did the photography captured that aspect perfectly."

"Most likely the photographer was Matthew Brady, although it could have been one of his staff." Benning grinned wryly. "That scoundrel never gives credit to his underlings, you know."

"The beast."

The two men chuckled.

"Perhaps you ought to start a studio in Blaineton, Carson. You could hire a few photographers to work with you. See where it goes."

Carson chuckled. "And become a scoundrel, too? We already have one of those in our town."

"My good man..." Benning clapped him on the shoulder again. "I doubt you ever could be a scoundrel."

The two shared a smile.

After a pause, Benning said softly, "Do remember to come back and visit me, won't you?"

"I shall, my friend. And once I start my own studio, I would like you to come and visit me."

"I shall. Never fear."

#

When Frankie and Patrick found their way to the Floral Department, they toured the two exhibits containing re-created arctic and tropical environments.

Then they spent time standing on the bridge over the fish pond and chatting.

"Which of the two zones did you like best?" Patrick asked of their visit to the displays.

"The Arctic Zone! I thought it was thrilling to see a ship trapped in the ice. And the lighting made it feel as if we were there! I mean, I could just imagine how the chill of the north wind would feel on my skin and could almost hear it howling."

"Well, I liked the Torrid Zone best. All those tropical plants and that Bengal tiger peeking through the leaves." Patrick grinned at his girl. "You can keep your frozen north. I'll take the tropics!"

Grasping the handrail on the bridge, Frankie leaned back and stared up at the ceiling. "After the war is over and we're married, perhaps we could live on an island in the Pacific Ocean. You would be the doctor there and I would preach."

"I understand they wear grass skirts." He took in her lithe form. "Would you put one of those on?"

"Maybe."

"I don't think the women wear anything on top."

"Patrick!" Frankie straightened up and let go of the railing. "That's rude!"

"Frankie, it's true! And you'd be beautiful like that."

She blushed scarlet. "Stop it."

Patrick laughed and pulled a pocket watch out of his jacket. "It's almost noon, honey. Let's go over to the restaurant and find the others."

#

The party enjoyed a delicious meal in the large, well-appointed restaurant, where the wait staff was comprised of young white ladies all dressed alike and men of color wearing black tail coats or white jackets. It was a busy place and the air was filled with the sound of voluminous voices, punctuated by laughter at regular intervals.

After they had eaten, the little group broke up once more to tour the rest of the Fair and to buy items to support the Sanitary Commission. Patrick bought Frankie a box of sweets, while Frankie and Lydia purchased little gifts for the family: candy, stationary, lithographs, and other souvenirs.

When the group left the Great Central Fair, they were glad to have spent their money to help the Commission and satisfied by the large, fascinating group of exhibits.

#

"When you get your next furlough," Frankie said to Patrick that night over a light supper at their hotel, "we ought to go to New York City. There are so many museums and art galleries we could see."

"We'll need to bring a chaperone."

"Of course." She studied him for a moment. "Pat, do you know how to draw?"

His brown eyebrows knit together over his blue eyes. "Why are you asking?"

"Because I can't. But after seeing all those paintings, I thought I might like to learn to draw. What about you?"

"I don't think I'd be very good at painting." Sometimes it was hard keeping up with the way her mind worked, but he loved her enthusiasm, something Philadelphia had caused to explode in joy. "But I can draw."

Her eyes widened. "Would you draw a picture of me?"

"Sure. When we're done eating, I'll get a piece of paper and a pencil. We'll sit in the lobby and I'll make a sketch of you."

Frankie nearly clapped her hands with joy. "I can't wait!"

83

"You make me laugh," he said, realizing how much he loved her. "I can't imagine not having you in my life."

She sat back in her chair. "I'll miss you, Pat."

When he reached a hand across the table to her, she smiled shyly and put her hand in his.

"I'll miss you, too, Frankie. Listen, I have something for you. Yesterday, while you and Lydia were taking a rest, I went out and bought this." Reaching into his pocket, he removed a small box and held it out to her.

Frankie was speechless as she took the box from him and opened it. Inside was a small silver ring set with a blue-tinted stone. Mouth agape, she looked up. "Pat..."

"It's a moonstone," he said. "It's like you, passionate. And it's like us, because it represents love." He took the box from her, removed the ring, and reached for her left hand.

"Oh, no!" his stunned girl sputtered. "Not that hand. That's where the wedding ring goes." She gave him her right hand instead. "Use this one."

Patrick slipped the ring on the appropriate finger and they stared at it for a moment.

"It's so beautiful!" Frankie murmured.

"*You're* beautiful," was his reply.

"I've never, ever had a ring before."

"Well, now you do. And it means we're officially promised to each other"

"I'll never take it off, Pat!"

He laughed. "I like the sentiment, but that stone might break if you wear it while you work. It's best to take it off when you wash the dishes, do the weeding, and such."

"Mama never takes off her wedding ring," Frankie said. "But that's a plain gold band. This ..." She held her hand up, so the stone caught the lamplight. "This is gorgeous!" She smiled broadly. "And don't worry, Patrick, I'll take good care of it." Then she added seductively,

"Just like I intend to take good care of you after we're married."

Patrick considered the intent of her words and tone. He grinned as he shook his head. "I don't think you have any idea what you mean, darling, but I'm looking forward to it!"

"Oh, I know what I mean." Her voice was throaty.

"You do?" Suddenly his voice had gone high, as if he were an insecure teenager. "That's... um... that's good."

Across the room, Lydia, Philip, and Carson surreptitiously watched the exchange.

"He gave her a ring," Lydia whispered. "How lovely!"

"I need to get *you* a ring," Philip said.

"You're a dear. But do take your time." She returned to her dish of strawberry ice cream. "I can wait."

"My darling girl, if this war has taught me one thing it's that we never know exactly how much time we have."

"I agree." Carson took a sip of coffee, relishing its dark, bitter flavor, and wondering how the hotel's restaurant got hold of it during wartime. "Perhaps you need to let Captain Frost decide what is the proper time for the ring, Lydia."

"Thank you, Mr. Carson. I shall." She turned to her husband, a smile on her face. "I will be delighted to receive a ring whenever you find the proper one."

"I intend to make that as soon as possible. Then," he leaned toward her across the table, "I will send you a wire and invite you for a weekend in Philadelphia."

"As soon as you are granted leave, that is."

He grinned. "As soon as I am granted leave."

Carson dabbed his lips with his napkin and placed it on the table. "I believe it is time for me to bid you two good night."

# Chapter 7: The Return

**12 June 1864**

The day Patrick and Philip were to report for duty at Mower General Hospital was difficult for both young couples. The little group of people arose that morning and had a quiet breakfast together. The men were dressed in their uniforms and ready to report, and the two young women worked hard not to notice too much.

After breakfast was over, Patrick and Philip returned to their rooms for their haversacks, while the others fetched their carpet bags. They met in the hall.

Frankie smiled bravely and took Patrick's arm. "You look very handsome today."

"I think all girls must say that to their fellas when they're in uniform."

"But you do look handsome," Lydia insisted. "Both of you."

Philip gave her a kiss on the cheek. "Well, you ladies look beautiful." Then he joked, "I fear our beauty will blind those around us!"

There was an awkward silence.

Philip took a breath. "Well, I suppose we ought to catch the train for Mower. No sense in delaying the inevitable."

The ride on the train did not take long, as it was only to Chestnut Hill. Frankie sat beside Patrick, holding his hand as she treasured these last minutes with him. Although it might be months before she saw him again, at least she felt at peace knowing he would not be on a battlefield.

In a seat across the aisle, Lydia sat with her head on Philip's shoulder. "As soon as you get a furlough, let me know," she murmured.

"Can you be away from your hospital for that long?"

She lifted her head and gazed into his eyes. "It depends on how many people are admitted and what their conditions are. Perhaps it might be best if you came to Blaineton."

He kissed the end of her nose. "I'd be happy to do that. I can think of nothing better than to be in that lovely, quiet little town."

Lydia chuckled. "It's not as quiet as you might think, but I would be delighted to have you there nonetheless."

All too soon the train jolted to a stop and its passengers began to file out. The couples stepped onto the platform and gazed at Mower General Hospital's front gate situated just up the path from them.

"Walk me down," Patrick said to his girl.

She smiled, took his hand, and went with him. Lydia and Philip did the same.

Smiling, Carson sat down on a bench, fished his pipe out of his pocket, lit it, and puffed contentedly as the four young people walked the path to the gate.

"Well," Patrick sighed when they reached the end of the path, "guess this is it."

Frankie nodded, not daring to speak for fear she would burst into tears.

He bent and kissed her on the lips. "I'll write as soon as I can, honey. Promise."

And then Frankie couldn't help herself. She threw her arms around his neck and hugged him tightly. "I love you," she whispered. After kissing him one last time, she stepped back.

Lydia and Philip were still sharing a tender kiss.

"I'll see you soon, darling," he whispered. "You've made me the happiest man on earth."

"And you've made me the happiest woman on earth," she replied.

"I don't know what the rest of your family will say when they find out we're married."

"I'll handle that. Don't worry." She kissed him once more. "I shall write every day."

"And I shall answer every day."

Philip turned, caught Patrick's eye, smiled faintly, and nodded in the direction of the hospital. The two then approached the gate, saluted the guard, presented their orders, and passed through as Lydia and Frankie looked on.

Once they were gone, Frankie pressed her lips together and struggled to keep from crying.

"Oh, now, it's going to be fine," Lydia whispered, taking her sister's arm in hers. "They're safe here and helping our wounded men. We are very lucky, Frankie. Very lucky, indeed."

#

Maggie surrendered Faith to Birgit and turned to her husband. "Are you ready?"

Eli was slapping his pockets in a desperate search for the dog-eared train schedule he carried around. "Almost."

"Why can't I come?" six-year-old Bob demanded.

"Because you're filthy, that's why," Eli muttered as he pulled the schedule out of his vest pocket. "You were clean this morning. I ought to know. I gave you a bath last night. Now you're not fit to go out in public. What do you and Natey do in your fort, anyway?"

"Fight the Johnnies," was the simple answer.

Natey nodded in agreement.

Maggie smiled, bent, and opened her arms. "Well, I don't care if you're dirty. Come here!"

88

Bob ran into her embrace and she kissed his dusty head. "But Papa's right. You'll have to wait to see Frankie and Lydia once they get home."

When she released him, Natey presented himself to her, demanding, "Me, too!"

Maggie hugged Emily and Nate Johnson's three-year old son and gave him a kiss. "There you go! Happy now?"

He nodded.

Eli glanced up from the schedule. "We need to go, sweetheart. The train is due in about thirty minutes."

Soon they were in the carriage and trundling down Greybeal Avenue toward the town of Blaineton. The sky was a bit overcast, but birds were singing, and a light breeze was keeping the humidity at bay.

Maggie glanced at her husband. "I hope they had a good time."

"Me, too."

"It was so odd."

Eli shook the reins and clucked at the horse. "Giddy-up!"

Romeo and Tybalt responded by picking up the pace.

"Everything's conspiring to slow us down today," he grumbled. Then he asked, "What was so odd, Maggie?"

"Seeing them leave with their beaus. It made me feel rather old."

He grinned. "Grandma."

"Elijah! I'm forty-three, not sixty-five!"

He laughed outright. "Oh, Maggie, Lydia and Frankie are growing up."

"Am I ready for young women instead of girls?" she mused.

Grinning, Eli nudged her with his shoulder. "I don't think your being ready has any bearing on it. They're becoming women whether you're ready or not."

#

The first one off the train was Carson. He set his carpet bag down, turned and received two other bags belonging to Lydia and Frankie. Then he held his hand out. Lydia took it and stepped down first. She was followed by Frankie.

Both sisters were glowing.

Maggie felt her heart quicken. She clearly could see something had happened. But she managed a welcoming smile and embraced her daughters.

Meanwhile, Eli noticed that Carson seemed terribly pleased. "What's the matter with you?"

Carson's smile lifted the ends of his white mustache. "I think I'll let the young ladies explain."

Narrowing his eyes, Eli studied his friend's face. "No. It's not them. It's you. Something is making *you* smile like that."

"Smile like what?"

"Like the cat that caught the canary."

"Ah. Well, I have a bit of news to share, but we'll leave that for later." And, still smiling, he marched off behind Lydia, Frankie, and their mother.

Eli grunted and followed. When he arrived at the carriage, the female members of the group were already seated, and all the carpet bags were on board and squeezed around his stepdaughters' feet.

Eli turned to his friend. "Hop up front between Maggie and me."

Carson shook his head. "No thank you, dear chap. It's a lovely day and I should like to walk back."

"Lovely day? Are you addlepated? It's clouded over!"

"Yes. I see that. Makes me relish a walk."

"Suit yourself. See you later." Eli clambered into the driver's seat and shook the reins.

As the horses plodded forward, Frankie leaned forward. "Papa?"

"Mm?"

90

"May we stop at Miss Amelia's Tea Shop?"

"What for?"

She hesitated. "Um... well..."

Lydia broke in, saying in a strong voice, "We need to tell you and Mama something."

Maggie turned in her seat and gazed quizzically at her daughters.

"Don't worry," Lydia assured her with a smile. "It's nothing awful."

"Oh. Well, thank goodness for that." She turned back around, now wondering – perhaps fearing – the news they had for her.

The carriage turned onto Second Street and passed the new hotel that now sat on the lot where Maggie's boarding house once stood. A few houses down the street, Eli parked and tethered the team to the hitching post in front of the tea shop, while Maggie, Lydia, and Frankie hopped down and entered the building.

By the time he got inside, the women were nowhere to be seen. Eli spotted Judith, Miss Amelia's assistant. She was carrying a pot of hot tea, a pitcher of cream, and a bowl of sugar on a tray. "Where did my family get to, Judith?" he asked.

She smiled. "They requested a private room, Mr. Smith." She nodded toward a door to the left of the room. "Follow me."

Eli trailed after her and took a seat beside his wife as Judith laid out the tea things.

"We ordered slices of the lemon cake," Maggie told her husband.

"Why did we get a private room?" he asked.

"Tea, Papa?" Frankie asked, as Judith left the room.

"Yes, please." He watched her pour the golden liquid into his cup. "What is it you wanted to talk to us about? And why in here?"

91

The two young women met each other's eyes and took a simultaneous breath.

"Well," Lydia began, "we thought it would be better here than at Greybeal House and since this is a public place, well, we thought a private room was called for."

Eli frowned slightly. "Well, then, go ahead. Talk. Spill the corn."

Frankie said, "While we were in Philadelphia, some significant things happened to the both of us."

Maggie stirred her tea, steeling herself.

"You see," Frankie continued, "Patrick –"

"Your lemon cake," Judith interrupted, arriving with another tray.

Disconcerted, Maggie murmured, "Thank you."

Eli watched Judith set the plates before them. She smiled pleasantly and departed, allowing Eli to return his eyes to Frankie. "Go on."

"Patrick gave me a gift." She held her hand out.

Maggie's mouth dropped open. Speechless, she reached for her daughter's hand.

"He... gave you that?" Eli stammered.

"Why, it's beautiful," Maggie exclaimed.

"My birthstone," Frankie burbled. "It's a moonstone! I love it."

Eli pursed his lips. "What was the occasion?"

"Engagement."

Maggie's mouth went dry. "A *marriage* engagement?"

Frankie giggled. "Is there any other kind?" She moved her hand, so Eli could see the ring better.

"Huh," he grunted. "That young pup spent a fair amount on it, didn't he?"

"Oh, Papa!" She pulled her hand back. "Don't be that way."

Maggie found her voice now. "Yes, Eli. Patrick is a fine young man. He's not some strange interloper. We've known him for years!"

Lifting her chin, Frankie added, "Pat bought it all by himself. And he even got the size right on the first try. Can you imagine? He knows me so well!"

"Yes, I can see he does," Eli relented. "Frankie, I want you to know that no matter what I may say about him, I have full confidence in Patrick. It's just old habits die hard." He reached for his stepdaughter's hand. She laid her hand on his and he added, "You have my solemn word: I believe Patrick will make you a fine husband."

The smile she rewarded him with said he had found the right words and had revealed what was in his heart and mind.

Maggie put her hand on top of theirs. "Frances, I am so happy for you. I think we all have known this would happen someday. I'm glad you chose Patrick."

"Thank you, Mama."

When they sat back in their seats, Maggie picked up her fork and tasted the lemon cake. It was delicious as usual. After she swallowed, she asked, "When do you anticipate having the wedding?"

"Oh, not until Patrick is mustered out," was the breezy reply.

The news gave her mother a strange sense of relief. She had the impression that once Patrick and Frankie were married, her daughter might move away from Greybeal House, from Blaineton, and from her. At least, Maggie told herself, she would have her little red-haired elf for another year, perhaps a bit more.

Then Frankie said, "Your turn, Liddy."

"Oh... yes..." her sister stammered. "Well, I must explain... that is, I must tell you that... I... we..."

Maggie and Eli waited.

"You see, while we were in Philadelphia..." her voice trailed away again.

Maggie asked, "For goodness sake, Liddy, what is it?"

Lydia blushed and self-consciously put her hands to her cheeks. "I've gone all red, haven't I?"

"You have." Maggie added easily, "But it is fine. Tell us what happened, please."

After taking her hands from her face, Lydia stared down at the polished tabletop. She took an unsettled breath. "Mama, Papa... while in Philadelphia, Philip and I..." She faded out again.

Eli dark eyebrows knit. "Philip and you what?"

"We... ah... well... we..."

"Oh, for heaven's sake, they got married," Frankie finished.

There followed a full minute of stunned silence.

Maggie was the first to speak. "Married?"

Lydia nodded. "Married."

"Just like that?"

"Yes."

"But you've known him not a year."

"Eleven months," Lydia corrected stubbornly. "I've known Philip for eleven months."

"Whose idea was it?" Eli's eyebrows were now fully knit together, and Lydia could see a storm was coming. "Did he push you into anything? Because if he did I'm gonna –"

"No, Papa!" Lydia straightened her shoulders. "It wasn't like that at all. No one pushed anybody into anything."

Maggie still was trying to digest the news. "But why? Why did you get married so suddenly, and not at home?"

"I know it seems sudden, Mama, but the truth is Phil and I have corresponded for nearly a year. During that time, we've shared our hearts, our philosophies, our hopes."

"I knew you had made amends before we left Middletown, but I did not think... that is, I had no idea..."

94

"I know I didn't share my feelings openly with you," Lydia confessed.

"You did not. Not at all! Don't you trust me?" Seeing the stunned look at her daughter's face, Maggie softened. "I'm sorry, Liddy."

"I had to be sure about this, Mama."

Maggie sighed. "You have always been hesitant to share things you aren't certain about."

"Unlike Frankie," Eli muttered. "She tells us everything, whether or not we want to know."

"Oh," was Frankie's tart reply. "Do neither of us please you, Papa?"

"Now, now," Lydia murmured. "That's not what he means. I believe Eli is saying that you've always been more forthcoming than I. I should think having two very different personalities would be a challenge to any parent."

Maggie offered an apologetic smile. "I never have regretted the way either of you are. You both are so precious to me, and I love you very much. But I must admit this has taken me by surprise."

A chastised Eli started at his cup. "I feel the same way." As he splashed some milk into the tea, he said, "I'm sorry, Liddy, Frankie. I spoke out of turn."

"We forgive you, Papa," Frankie said.

Lydia returned to reassuring her mother. "Let me explain. Over the past months, Phil and I shared the things that were important in our lives: a love of family, country, and medicine. We had discussed working together as physicians when he was mustered out. Our friendship grew over that time. I knew Phil had been interested in pursuing more than friendship with me, but the loss of Edgar was too acute at that time."

"What changed?" Maggie asked.

"I found Philip more and more companionable over time. And then..." Her eyes filled with tears. "Then I had

95

a dream while we were in Philadelphia. Edgar was in it and he told me I needed a partner, that I shouldn't be afraid, and if I hesitated I may never have another chance."

Maggie's eyes teared up, too. How many times had she dreamed of John Blaine? How many times had he come back to reassure her, to give her hope? Perhaps the dear departed sought to help those left behind. It was a comforting thought.

"While we were in Philadelphia, Phil and I realized how much we loved each other. And then we attended the concert at that lovely church and Phil said it would be a fine place in which to be wed. I agreed and... well, after the concert we asked the minister if he would marry us."

"You couldn't have waited until you got back to Blaineton?"

"Oh, Mama, waiting is fine for some." Lydia's voice was soft. "But the time was right. We have not made a mistake, Mama. I love him, and he loves me."

Maggie's heart melted. She knew what it was like to make a quick decision. And impulsiveness was one of the hallmarks of being young. But Maggie also understood that in the preceding months, Lydia had done what she had always done: thought things over long and hard before she came to a decision.

Maggie reached across the table once more. "Give me your hand, my dear."

Lydia did.

"May you and Philip have a long and happy life together. And may God bless your every endeavor." She smiled at Frankie now. "And may you and Patrick have a long and happy life, too. And may your endeavors bear fruit, too."

"Thank you, Mama," Lydia said.

"I hope you like grandchildren, Mama," Frankie teased. "Because we'll probably give you dozens!"

Lydia rolled her eyes heavenward. "Oh, not dozens! Please!"

#

Later that evening, Maggie was sitting on the front porch. A light rain was falling after the cloudy day. As she listened to the patter of the drops on the tree leaves, grass, and rooftop, she rocked a sleeping Faith. The sound of the raindrops was soft and soothing. At her feet, Bob had also fallen asleep. A dozen small, tin soldiers lay scattered around him.

"Beautiful night," Eli commented as he stepped onto the veranda.

Maggie smiled up at him. "It is."

"I like the rain." He took a seat in the rocking chair beside hers. "Momentous day wasn't it?"

"It seems almost yesterday that Frankie and Lydia were as small as Faith and Bob. I scarce can comprehend how they grew up so quickly."

Eli gazed at the baby in her arms. "I suspect that one day soon this little one will be a young woman." He nodded at Bob. "And this little fella will be a strapping young man. And then we'll wonder how it all happened."

Maggie sighed.

"It's life, Maggie. It's the way it should be."

She wiped tears from her eyes, unable to speak for the depth of the uncountable feelings swirling in her soul.

"What is it, sweetheart?"

Maggie took a breath. "Oh, I was remembering my little Gideon. He never got the chance to grow up. I wonder what he would be like had he lived?"

Eli's eyes met hers. "He would have been loving, kind, intelligent, and decent. Just like you."

She sniffed and wiped at her eyes again.

He dragged a handkerchief from a pocket and handed it to his wife.

Maggie nodded her thanks and mopped her eyes.

"You see, we don't notice the small changes," he said. "I think we don't *want* to see them. It seems as if children grow up overnight, but the truth is they don't. Not really."

Cradling Faith close to her bosom, Maggie whispered, "I was unprepared for how this would feel. I'm sure both my girls will be leaving and starting their families and lives away from us. I should be delighted, but it feels so hollow."

Eli leaned close and whispered, "Not hollow, my love. Not hollow. Just different." He gave her a gentle smile. "Have faith. All will be well."

"That's what I usually say to you," she replied in a small voice.

"We say things to others to encourage them, but sometimes, my love, we need to hear *others* say those things back to us."

His word brought a deep peace to her heart that spread throughout her body. "Elijah Smith, I love thee."

"And I love *thee*, Margaret Smith."

"And so, all well be well."

Eli nodded. "Yes, my love, all will be well."

# Notes & References

## Notes

Page 6: "Copperhead," a Northern Democrat who opposed the war and wanted an immediate peace with the Confederate States of America.


Page 31: "Slouch hat" – a wide-brimmed hat.


Page 34: "Kirkbride-style building" – a hospital for the insane designed by Dr. Thomas Story Kirkbride to accommodate a form of treatment called the Moral Treatment Method. "Careful attention was given to every detail of their design to promote a healthy environment and convey a sense of respectable decorum. Placed in secluded areas within expansive grounds, many of these insane asylums seemed almost palace-like from the outside. But growing populations and insufficient funding led to unfortunate conditions, spoiling their idealistic promise."
http://www.kirkbridebuildings.com/)


Pages 72-73: Frankie is quoting from the *Philadelphia Sanitary Fair Catalogue and Guide.* Thomas Izod, ed. (Philadelphia: Magee Stationer, June 1864.)

## Information on the cover image:

Title
The U.S. sanitary fair, Logan Square, Phila. 1864 / Frank H. Taylor after Queen.

# The Great Central Fair

# An Alternate Ending (Just for Fun)

One of my beta readers, Laura Wimbrow, is also a fan. To my surprise and delight, she sent me a piece of fan fiction. My very first fan fiction! I was thrilled

The ending is written in the style of a play. It struck me as so funny because Laura took my characters and ran to extremes with them.

*Laura wrote:*

I must admit that I formulated an "alternative ending," once Lydia and Philip were married. Of course, I love your ending; it's better and it's much more in character. But I envisioned this happening

*Laura's alternative ending:*

Maggie and Eli approach Chester on the platform, as the girls hang behind him. Maggie smiles in greeting at all three, and Eli claps Chester on the back.

Eli: Greetings, Carson! I see you managed to survive the journey none the worse for the wear. So, tell me, how did you and your young charges find Philadelphia?)

Chester: The city was as beautiful and enthralling as ever, and I dare say my young companions found it even more spellbinding. We took in the sights, ate many fine and delicious foods, thoroughly enjoyed the Fair, and two of our number were married by journey's end. Anyway,

I'll go see to the bags and leave you all to it. (He dashes off)

(a beat and a half of silence)

Maggie, as usual trying to process ten different feelings all at once: Did he say.... married? (long pause) Frances? Frances, I ... well, I always knew you were the impulsive one, but...married? Away from us? Frances, I am not sure I approve---

Eli: WHERE IS PATRICK. BRING PATRICK TO ME. I WANT TO MAKE HIM DEAD.

Frankie: Mama, Papa...it's not what you think---

Eli: SILENCE, GIRL. WHEN IS THE NEXT TRAIN TO MOWER? I AM GOING TO BE ON IT.

Maggie: Eli, calm yourself.

Eli: I WILL NOT BE CALMED. I TOLD THAT BOY!

Lydia: It was me.

Eli: TICKET WINDOW. I GO THERE NOW!

Lydia: Mama! Papa, listen, please! It was not Patrick and Frances who were married! It was Philip and I.

(long, long silence as everyone in the party slowly turns to face Lydia)

Lydia: Philip and I quietly married in a church in Philadelphia. May we please go somewhere a bit less public and I will share the details?

Maggie hugs Lydia, mostly out of relief that it was she who got married and not Frankie.

Eli visibly deflates and looks as though he could use a stiff drink and a long nap: "By God Above. Daughters will be the utter death of me."

## THE END

# About the Author

Janet Stafford is a Jersey girl, book lover and lifelong scribbler. She readily confesses to being overly-educated, having received a B.A. in Asian Studies from Seton Hall University, as well as a Master of Divinity degree and a Ph.D. in North American Religion and Culture from Drew University. Having answered a call to vocational, but non-ordained ministry, Janet has served six United Methodist Churches, working in spiritual formation, communications, and ministries with children, youth, and families. She also was an adjunct professor for six years, teaching college classes in interdisciplinary studies and world history.

Writing, history, and religion came together for Janet when she authored *Saint Maggie*, an historical novel set in 1860-61 and based on a research paper written during her Ph.D. studies. She thought the book would be a single novel, but kept hearing readers ask, "What happens next?" In response, Janet created a series that follows the unconventional family from the first book through three other novels and three short stories, all set in the traumatic years of the American Civil War.

Janet also ventured into the contemporary romance genre, going closer to home (the church) for her source material. *Heart Soul & Rock 'n' Roll* tells the story of 40-year-old Lindsay Mitchell, who led a rock band in college but for the past fifteen years has worked as an assistant minister. Besieged by a mid-life crisis, Lins wonders if perhaps she isn't called to something new. But could that "something new" be a relationship with Neil, a man with a messy life and a bar band called the Jersey Reapers?

www.ingramcontent.com/pod-product-compliance
Lightning Source LLC
Chambersburg PA
CBHW020152180626
46810CB00004B/1861